The Red Headed Girl

Published by Coles-Cumberland Press

ISBN: 978-0-930893-07-1

Dedication

To Sharon Wertz
I couldn't have done it without you.

Table of contents

Preface

My name is Seamus Ryan Sanford... my twin sister Shannon and I were only two when we came west on the last Orphan Train in 1929. I found out about her when my adoptive mother wrote to the Foundling Hospital where we were born. Our mother died a few days after our birth, but we lived at the Foundling Hospital for two years until the Orphan Train brought us to Illinois. Now that I knew about her, I set off to find my twin sister...

One: I Go To Marshall

The lump in my throat felt as big as a clod of new plowed ground, and my eyes were fighting tears. A fourteen-year-old boy is too old to cry just because he's going to be away from his folk for a whole school year.

"I knew it would be hard, Shamie," my sister said, "but you're going to be fine."

I nodded my head but couldn't trust myself to say anything. Then I heard old Duke barking in the back yard and remembered Stormy. She's my cat I brought from the farm. I knew she'd probably pushed her way out of the screen door on the back porch. I ran around the side of the house and unlatched the heavy iron gate. As I opened it, I saw Stormy race up the oak tree by the carriage house. Duke stood his ground, barking like all get out. Stormy had clawed his nose something awful.

"Come on, old boy. Let's put some Rawleigh salve on your nose." Together, we went up the back steps where Livy was waiting.

"I see Stormy met Duke," she laughed and petted the dog.

"I hope she'll settle down and get along with him like she does with Bobbie." I was feeling a little sad just thinking about home as I sat down next to Livy. We didn't say much for a while as we watched the wind blow the yellowing leaves on the oak tree.

Finally, Livy looked over at me and sighed. "I hope you aren't sorry you said you'd help me while the Ashleys are in Washington. I'm not much good at looking after horses."

"Yeah, I know." I had to laugh at Livy. She was born on a farm, but she doesn't know much about the work. "I'll have a good time with the horses. And all the money they're paying me for the yard work and taking care of the horses will be more'n enough for my school expenses. Besides, I bet you'd be scared to stay in this big house by yourself?"

"Well," Livy grinned, "you may be right. I'll admit that taking care of those horses isn't the only reason I wanted you here." She sighed like Mother does when she's feeling edgy about something. "Remember when Mother talked about her year of teaching back in 1907 and all those silly rules teacher had to follow? Like not engaging in any unseemly conduct like getting married."

"Yeah, that's hard to believe in 1941, isn't it?"

"Oh, most of the rules have changed, but not what people think. Now that I'm principal of North Grade School, I could do things that would upset people. Just one nasty comment could start a story that would hurt my reputation."

I thought about that while I looked at my sister. She's awful pretty with long brown hair and blue eyes that sparkle with fun. Her skin looks like the picture on the Ivory soap wrapper. I couldn't bear to think about anyone saying bad things about her. "They'd better not say anything while I'm around," I said.

"Now don't get mad," Livy laughed.

"When I lived in the carriage house apartment last year, Regina and Fredrick were here and nobody would dare say anything about me. She knows everyone one in town and how much money they have."

"I guess she's pretty rich, huh?"

"Well, yes, but people respect her and are half afraid of her at the same time. Her grandfather founded this town, and as the bank president, she's done a lot for it. Even though women have had the vote for over twenty years, we still aren't taken seriously. I would never have gotten the principal's job if Regina hadn't stood up to the board and told them it was time they started living in the 20th Century. There are some men on that school board who would love to see me fail."

"Well, they'd better be careful."

"That's right, little brother," she said ruffling my hair.

"I'm glad you talk to me like I was growed up. I mean, like I was grown up," I said, correcting myself.

"I'm proud of you, Shamie. You've matured so much this year, and your grammar has improved, too. What caused that?"

"When I started high school at Toledo last fall, I listened to some of the kids talk, I thought they sounded pretty sorry, then I heard myself. Even Mary Ruth told me I sounded like a hick. She don't care what she says." I knew I'd made another blunder, but Livy just laughed and didn't say a word. "I hope you'll correct me when we're by ourselves, but..."

"I understand. It will get easier."

"I reckon so," I said hoping I didn't embarrass her with my country talk. "What did you sign me up for at school?"

"Well," Livy started out, "you may not like your schedule, but I put you in classes you'll need in college. Classes I should've had."

"What's that?"

"Well, first of all, I asked Miss Greathouse if you could take beginning typing. She didn't want to at first."

"But at Toledo, we have to be juniors to take it."

"I know, but honestly, Shamie, your handwriting is so hard to read. You'll be glad I talked her into letting you audit the class. You'll see how much better your grades will be if teachers can read your work."

I knew my handwriting wasn't pretty, but I could read it. Well, most of the time. Even though I skipped the fifth grade, I'm nowhere near as smart as she thinks I am. While I was thinking about the typing, Livy went into the room she calls the office and brought back my schedule. Geometry, English, science, typing and Spanish. I guess I must have looked dumb struck when I said, "Spanish?"

"It'll be a lot easier for you at fourteen than it was for me when I started college. I'll be able to help you. And besides, Mr. Vadas is really sweet and patient," she said. "Come on, I want to show you the office where you'll do your studying. There's even a typewriter."

"Really? Where'd you get it?"

"It's Regina Ashley's. She cleaned everything out of her desk so you could use it." Livy said, pulling on my arm. "Come on."

Dad and me had looked over the stable and the other buildings when we first got here, but I hadn't seen much of the house except my bedroom. So naturally I was curious about the office. It was in the back corner of the house just off the porch where we were sitting. What took my eye was the old desk that was between the two back windows.

"Wow, look at that desk. I bet it's really old," I could hardly believe that I was going to have this whole room to myself.

Livy nodded. "It belonged to Regina's grandmother. She was quite a lady, and I've heard she was a friend of Abraham Lincoln's. But half the people in Marshall say that," she laughed and ran her hand over the dark wood of the desk. "It's a Chippendale."

"I wonder if it has any secret compartments."

"With all that fancy scroll work it would be hard to find."

"I've never been in a room like this," I said. "You reckon I'll get used to it and be able to study in it?"

"I know what you mean. It's hard to believe all these lovely antiques. You can see why Regina wanted someone she trusted to look after her things."

"I sure can," I said, and then I eased down careful-like in the leather chair. When I swiveled around I noticed the typing desk was close enough to reach from the chair. I just hoped I really could learn to type.

After a while Livy took me on a tour of the house, all fifteen rooms. Of course that was counting the pantry and front hall that was big enough to hold a dance in. Every room seemed fancier than the next, but I didn't like any of them as much as the office. There were five bedrooms and a big bathroom upstairs. On the third floor there was another bedroom. I figured it was for a maid. There was also a playroom that hadn't been used for ages, and Livy said I could practice karate there.

The thing that surprised me most was the big furnace in the basement that could heat the whole house. There was a laundry room, a place to store canned goods and bins for apples, potatoes and other stuff from the garden. Along the back wall I noticed notched shelves with bottles laying in 'em. I asked Livy why they needed so much catsup, and she just about died laughing. When she finally stopped, she told me the bottles had wine in them. I knew for sure she hadn't showed this part of the basement to Mother.

After supper we listened to the big Philco radio and record player combination in the library. It was a console model and electric, so I wouldn't have to worry about the batteries running down like on the farm. I saw one almost like it in the Sears catalog, and it cost $129.99.

We listened to "The Shadow" and the "First Nighter," the programs I look forward to on Sunday night. Naturally, before we turned the radio off, we heard more about the war in Europe. I sure feel sorry for those folks in London with the German planes bombing them so bad.

When Livy turned the radio off, she said we'd better eat a little ice cream before we went to bed, and that did seem to make me feel better. While we ate, Livy talked a little more about my twin sister, Shannon.

To tell you the truth, Shannon's the real reason I wanted to come to Marshall. A family here adopted her when she was two, the same time my folks took me in twelve years ago. We came to Illinois from New York on the Orphan Train with a lot of other kids. But I didn't know I had a twin sister until the

Rawleigh man told me there was a redheaded girl in Marshall that was a spittin' image of me.

That was four years ago, but Shannon doesn't know about me. Livy and me have talked about whether or not we should tell her, but she left that up to Shannon's father, Judge Richard Williams. Livy thought I ought to meet Shannon before school started because I'll be sure and see her there this year. Since this is her great aunt's house, Livy didn't think Shannon was surprised that she'd invited her for lunch tomorrow.

It was after ten o'clock when I went to my room. Livy thought I'd like it because it was at the head of the back stairs that led directly to the kitchen. It would be handy in case I got hungry at night. Mother says I have two hollow legs because I'm always hungry. But that doesn't surprise her since I'm growing so fast. I grew nearly three inches last year, making me six feet tall. Dad says I look like a long legged colt, but he expects I'll shape up before I've finished growing. With all the excitement of meeting Shannon tomorrow, I had a mighty hard time falling asleep.

The Red Headed Girl

Two: My First Day in Marshall

When I woke up next morning, I heard Livy down in the kitchen banging pans around. At first I couldn't think where I was, but when I saw the four-poster bed I remembered. It seemed funny having a bathroom right outside my room, but I figured I'd get used to that in a hurry. I wouldn't miss that long walk to the outhouse on the farm.

Livy called good morning to me when I came into the kitchen. I was wearing my old overalls without a shirt. I was glad it was Labor Day, and I had a little time to get acquainted with the horses. They're not farm horses like ours, so they require more care. One thing for sure, they need to drink water before they're fed or they'll swell up.

When I went out on the porch to look at the new day, I found Stormy in the little house I made for her when she was just a kitten. I'd made it nice and snug and lined it with an old rug. When she saw me, she opened her eyes, stretched and started to follow me down to the stable. She changed her mind when Duke came out of his house and began barking.

After I let the horses out of the stable and pumped some water for 'em I went back to the kitchen for breakfast. I could see that cooking would be a lot faster on that big gas range, and I wouldn't need to bring in kindlin' or firewood for it. And best of all, there wouldn't be all those ashes to carry out.

"How were Blaze and Star this morning?" Livy asked me as I walked across the kitchen to wash my hands at the sink.

"Anxious to get a drink. Old Duke barked at their heels a-trying to help me, but I noticed he stayed out of hoof range."

"Sit down," she said. You'll have to make do with toast this morning."

"Toast is fine," I told her. "You fried the bacon just the way I like it." Livy poured coffee in both our cups and put the pot back on the stove.

"I hope you don't get homesick for the cream separator," she said, serious-like when she handed me a half-pint bottle of store-bought cream. I didn't know what to make of it 'til I saw the sparkle in her eyes. She knew how much I dreaded washing the cream separator and turning it night and morning.

"I don't reckon I will," I mumbled with my mouth full of food.

After breakfast I washed the dishes and fixed a plate of scraps for Stormy while Livy made a tuna casserole for lunch. She told me how to work the gas stove and when to put the food in the oven. Before she left for the office, she reminded me about setting the table and changing my clothes. She sounded like Mother, but I guess ladies are just natural-born bosses and think men probably need to be reminded about everything. After I was clear on all my instructions, I headed back out to feed the horses.

The stable looks like one of those fancy barns where racehorses live in Kentucky only a lot smaller. One end has a good size tack room where bales of hay and sacks of grain are stored along with the saddles and other equipment. On the other end are two box stalls with doors that open out into the stable yard. When I got there, the horses were by the water tank, but they came right in when they saw me putting alfalfa out for them.

After they finished eating, I cleaned the stalls. By ten o'clock I'd finished my work, and decided to exercise the horses in the pasture. It must have been at least five acres, and the land sloped down to a little creek where there was a small grove of trees. After the horses and I got acquainted, I wanted to ride over to the fairground where it would be safe to race around the track.

I saddled Star, but just put a bridle on Blaze and led him along while I trotted Star around the pasture. After I thought they'd had enough exercise, I brought them back to the stable and was brushing them when I heard someone calling from the yard.

"Hello out there. Anyone home?"

I looked out the stable door, and there stood the prettiest girl I'd ever seen. I knew it was Shannon the minute I saw her, but where was Livy? I was supposed to be all cleaned up wearing my new school clothes by the time Shannon got here.

It was too late to do anything else, so I stuck my head out and called, "I'm in the stable." The next thing I heard the gate bang, and there was my twin sister standing in the open half door staring at me.

"Are you the new stable boy?" She asked it like a high-toned lady that wanted her horse brought to the front gate.

"Well, I-I guesses I am. My name is Seamus."

"You look familiar. Do I know you?"

"No, I don't reckon you do, not unless you can count being pen pals for a while when I was ten."

She looked puzzled for a while before she answered. "Oh, yes. Seamus Sanford. I used to write to you. Miss Sanford told me about her brother, but I didn't think you were the same one."

I just nodded my head, but words stuck in my throat. I guess I'm not very memorable. I'd wondered for three years why Shannon had stopped writing to me. I wrote two more times after she stopped, and then I gave up. Finally I asked, "Where's Livy? Didn't she bring you?"

"No, I rode my bike over because I'm going to play tennis with my friend this afternoon. Miss Sanford will be here pretty soon."

"Oh, my! She told me to put the casserole in the oven at eleven thirty. Do you know what time it is?"

Shannon looked at her dainty gold watch and said, "It's just about that time."

By now, I'd curried both horses more than they needed, so I couldn't stay in the stable any longer. I opened the bottom half of the door and went outside. I could feel my face getting hot. If only I'd paid more attention to the time and got cleaned up before Shannon got here!

"I'm sorry I'm such a mess," I said, rubbing my sweaty hands on my overalls just in case she wanted to shake hands. But she had hers stuck in the pockets of her white shorts, looking at me like she'd never seen a boy wearing overalls before.

"My goodness," she said, "you don't look a bit like Miss Sanford."

"Well, no. I'm adopted, so I don't look like any of the family."

"I'm adopted, too, but hardly anyone knows. My mother had strawberry blonde hair, but mine's a little darker."

We stood there sizing one another up, and I wondered if she could see that we looked a lot alike. Her hair wasn't as curly as mine and not quite as red, but her eyes were the same color of dark blue. I knew she didn't see me, she saw my dirty overalls and old clodhopper shoes. I was just the stable boy. At least since I've been leaving my shirt off this summer, I didn't have a red neck.

She was wearing a blue shirt that matched her eyes, and her hair was long and wavy. It was streaked with gold and copper lights and she wore it loose like that movie star, Veronica Lake, half over one side of her face. Finally, I asked, "You want to sit on the porch while I get cleaned up? Livy will skin me alive if she sees me like this."

She nodded and we walked up the path without saying anything. When we opened the screen door, Stormy woke up, stretched herself and bowed graceful-like, her white fur shining in the sun.

"Oh what a beautiful cat," Shannon exclaimed. "Is she yours?"

"Yeah. Her name is Stormy, and I brought her from the farm. She doesn't like anyone but me very much, so I'd be careful of her," I said. Then I hurried into the kitchen to put the casserole in the oven and on upstairs to clean up.

By the time Livy got home, I'd set the table, and the casserole was beginning to smell good. Most important, I was cleaner 'n a whistle, wearing my new school clothes. But I was still uneasy. After all this time of wanting to meet my twin sister, I didn't know what to make of her.

The Red Headed Girl

Three: My Twin Comes to Lunch

I was mighty glad when lunch was over because I'd felt uneasy ever since we started to eat. I didn't say more than two words, but that was because it was just girl talk between Livy and Shannon. Livy tried to bring the conversation around to stuff I'm interested in, but that didn't work. Shannon wanted to talk about her summer in Chicago with her grandparents, her ballet recital and all the rich people she met.

Things like karate, the guitar and running didn't seem to interest her. I was so fidgety I didn't feel much like eating, and that's mighty unusual for me. When I went to the kitchen to get more iced tea I heard Shannon ask Livy if I was always so quiet, but I didn't hear her answer.

Since I'm not used to taking ice cubes out of those little trays and refilling them, I was quite a while getting back to the dining room. I was surprised to see Shannon was getting ready to leave. I heard her talking to Livy real fast, like she was trying to get out in a hurry. I figured it was because she didn't want to talk to me again.

"Tell Seamus goodbye for me," Shannon smiled at Livy as they walked toward the front hall. "I really do have to hurry." Even from where I was standing in the dining room, I could see her smile was the polite kind, the kind that only shows on your lips. I didn't want my first meeting with Shannon to end like this, so I hurried to the front door.

"Thanks for coming, Shannon," I said, "If you ever want to go horseback riding, just whistle." When Livy saw me, she said goodbye to Shannon and went into the library. That left me and Shannon standing awkward-like in the front hall.

The minute Livy closed the library door, Shannon's smile faded completely. She looked me right in the eyes and said, "I don't care for riding, Seamus." She nodded her head like she'd settled that. "Your sister asked me to introduce you to my friends, but I don't think they'd have much in common with you." Then she said goodbye and walked down the steps to her bike. I was surprised when she didn't head toward the park until I noticed she didn't have a tennis racket. I felt a part of my world crumble.

Later, when Livy came into the kitchen, I'd washed the dishes and was watching Stormy lap up milk from a bowl while I strummed my guitar. Before I brought her in, I'd made sure she couldn't escape into the rest of the house and get her sharp claws into that fancy furniture.

Stormy was concentrating on her milk and not paying much attention to me. She's a real independent cat, and I'm just about the only human she puts up with. That's the reason I had to bring her along. The folks tease me about my stuck-up cat, but I guess she can't help being the way she is any more than Shannon can.

I was so busy telling Stormy my troubles I hardly heard Livy open the door until she asked, "Is this a private concert, or may I listen?" Then she came on in and looked around the clean kitchen. "Thanks for doing the dishes, Shamie," she said, and put her hand on my shoulder. "I don't know what made Shannon act so awful today." Then she heaved a big sigh and said, "I need to blow off some steam. Let's go for a run around the high school track."

"Sounds good to me. I'd like to see the school."

"It's only eight blocks from here, but let's take the car so I can show you around town before we run."

"I'll go change into my old gym shorts," I said, picking up Stormy and putting her on the porch. I wanted her to get used to the new place before I let her out on her own.

While I was changing, Livy went to the garage to get the car. Yesterday when Dad and me looked in there, I saw her car next to the Ashley's big Chrysler, and it looked kind of sad. But Livy is so glad to have a car, she doesn't care if the paint's scratched and the fenders have a few dents in them. She got it for practically nothing from Aunt Mary and Uncle Edward when they bought a new car last year. Livy's car is a 1935 Chevrolet coupe and sold for $475 when it was new. Even though it's six years old, it runs like a top. It has brand new tires because Uncle Edward was going to keep it another year, but he decided to get a new car while the getting was good. With all the auto factories being made into defense plants, he knew he'd have to wait a long time to get another car.

It wasn't long until Livy drove into the circle drive where I was waiting. She grinned at me as I opened the door and climbed in. Then she tooted the horn so I could hear it "uh-oo-ga" as we turned into the street. After that, she concentrated on her driving while I looked out the window.

Since the town was new to me, I paid close attention to the way we were going, watching the street signs as we passed. We drove down Beech Street to Third, and south to the business district on Archer. Then she turned south and drove around the square so I could see the Clark County courthouse.

It's a real nice red brick building with a clock tower on top. A big bandstand's on the northeast corner of the square, and Livy says there's a band concert every Friday night during summer. When we turned back on Archer, she pointed out the Grabenhumer Building where Lincoln made a speech once, and then on past the Candy Kitchen, the place the kids get together for Cherry Cokes and stuff. By then we were at the intersection of Archer and Route One where we had to stop for the light.

While we waited to turn left, Livy pointed out the city water tower behind the National Dixie Hotel. "You can see the tower all over town," she said, "and if you get lost, you can get your bearings from it."

I just grinned and reminded her, "I'm not the one that gets lost, Livy. That's you."

She looked at me kind of sheepish-like and shrugged her shoulders but didn't say any more. I was busy watching the street signs, so I didn't say anything either. Most of the streets going east and west are named for trees like Maple and Oak, but the ones going north and south have numbers. Even though the town's a lot bigger than Toledo, I figured it would be easy to get around in from the way it was laid out. Finally, Livy turned east on Hickory, then on to Eighth. On the corner of Spruce and Eighth were two big red brick houses. They were really something!

She slowed down and pointed out Shannon's house. "The one across the street is where the Radcliffes live. Janet's father owns the Ford agency here." A big convertible that looked like it had cost aplenty was parked in the driveway. It was the kind of car that belonged with a fancy house, and it made me think of seeing Dad's old pickup truck in front of the Ashley's house yesterday. I guessed that's what Shannon meant when she said I wouldn't have anything in common with her friends. She couldn't picture me wearing anything but faded overalls.

A little later when Livy pulled into a parking place in front of the high school, I took a good look at it. The building had towers on either side of the wide front doors, and little toadstool-like caps with windows all around topped them. I didn't know what style of architecture it was supposed to be, but it kind of reminded me of the Parliament Building in London. Not that I've ever been there, but I've seen pictures of it. The walls of the school had ivy growing over them, and I thought the green leaves looked real nice on the red brick.

"That's a lot fancier than Toledo High," I said to Livy as we walked across the lawn. She was looking out toward the football field at a girl running around the track, so she wasn't paying much attention to me.

"That's Janet Radcliffe. I didn't realize she was a runner," Livy commented as we walked toward the bleachers. She put her purse and jacket on the bench and grinned at me. "Race you around the track," she said, and took off before I had time to answer.

Livy's a pretty good runner, but I could tell she was out of practice. I didn't want to pass her too soon, so I made sure my shoestrings were tied before I started after her. As I got into a steady rhythm, I speeded up. By the time I was nearly around I passed her by the place we'd started. She grinned and waved at me as I went by. The next time I came around, Livy was sitting on the bench talking to Janet Radcliffe. The first thing I noticed about Janet was how long her legs were. They were tan and 'most as skinny as mine. Maybe the bloomers of her green gym suit made them look thinner. Not that I know a lot about girls' clothes, but I was sure it was a gym suit because no girl would buy it unless she had to.

Since I was just getting warmed up, I waved at Livy and went around the track again. While running I'd been thinking about the sports here, wondering if I could make the track team. I've been running since I was ten, and Dad says I'm a natural. I couldn't be on the track team last year because I had to catch a ride home with some neighbor kids right after school.

By the time I came around again, Livy waved at me to stop. "Seamus, I want you to meet Janet Radcliffe. She says she's going out for the girl's track team."

"Hi, Seamus," Janet said, real friendly-like. "You're really fast."

"Thanks. Are you practicing already?" I picked up my towel and wiped the sweat off my face before I sat down.

"Can't get too much practice," Janet smiled at me. She had the brownest eyes I'd ever seen, and they just matched her long hair pulled back in a ponytail. She was real pretty, and I liked the way her eyes lit up like she was happy to be talking to me. After a while, she had to go. "I'm glad to meet you, Seamus," she said, getting up from the bleacher. "I'll see you at school tomorrow." She started to leave, and then she turned back and looked at me. "Miss Sanford says you're a sophomore."

"Yeah, and I'm excited about coming here," I said. Livy kind of nudged me in the ribs, and I remembered I was supposed to stand up when girls do. Livy has been coaching me on my manners, and my best friend Mary Ruth kept reminding me last year at Toledo. Between them, I'm not quite as big a clod about manners as I used to be. "See you tomorrow," I said, wondering if she'd be this nice when she was with her friends.

After she walked away Livy told me more about her. "She and Shannon have been friends since first grade."

"She seems real nice," I said, wondering why Shannon thought I wouldn't have anything in common with her friends.

"She is, but she's pretty shy. At least she was last year when I substituted a while in eighth grade after the teacher was drafted into the army. Poor guy, he'd just finished college, and he only got to teach a few months."

We were back at the car when Livy remembered to tell me she'd received a letter from Mr. Smith, my grade school teacher. He was going to join the navy because he didn't want to get drafted, but the draft board deferred him until he finished his last class and graduated from college.

Livy smiled at me and said, "He asked me to say hello to you. He's glad you're going to be here with me this year."

I think Mr. Smith is sweet on Livy because he seemed to show up at our house every time she came home for the weekend.

On the way home we drove past the Clark County Fairground so I could see the racetrack. The swimming pool and park are right close, and a lot of folks were enjoying the last day of the summer season at the pool.

I was about to ask Livy more about Mr. Smith's letter when I saw Shannon and a dark- haired guy getting out of the pool. "Oh, there's Shannon."

"I see her. That's Derek Radcliffe, Janet's brother. He's a senior this year and quite the lady's man I hear. No wonder Shannon was in such a hurry to leave."

"Yeah, I guess so." I wondered why she didn't just say she had a date. After all she didn't have to come to lunch. I couldn't help feeling a little jealous looking at Derek's wide shoulders. "He's built like a football player," I said, wondering if I'd ever fill out and have shoulders like his.

Livy slowed down and waved. To make sure Shannon saw us, she tooted the horn a couple times. Sometimes Livy reminds me of Dad with his teasing.

When we got home, I was surprised to see a little old man picking tomatoes in the garden. "What's he doing in your garden?" It's a good thing I'm here to take care of Livy.

"Oh, that's Jimmy Black. The Ashleys let him care for the garden, and he takes what he wants. He lives in a little shack over by the fairground and barely makes ends meet on his military pension. Come on, I'll introduce you. He's quite an interesting character."

Jimmy looked up and grinned when he saw us walking down the flagstone path toward the garden. "Howdy, Miss Sanford. Is this your little brother you've been bragging about?"

"It sure is." Livy put her arm around my waist and gave me a little hug. "Seamus, this is Jimmy Black. He used to be a jockey on the fair circuit before the World War."

I stuck my hand out, and he took it. "Hi, Jimmy. Do you still ride?" When Livy said jockey, I forgot all about my worries about him, thinking I might learn something about horses.

"Not any more. I'm too stove up to get on a horse," he laughed kind of sad-like. "It's all I can do to walk these days. My racin' days was finished when that bullet hit me in the knee cap over in France."

"I'm mighty sorry," I said. "I sure like to ride. Maybe you could tell me something about your racing days."

"Sure enough." he grinned. Your sister says you're here to look after the Ashley's horses. Ride over to the track some day, and we'll have us a good visit." He picked up three ripe tomatoes from a pile on the ground and handed them to Livy. "These should be tasty for your supper," he said, putting the rest of the tomatoes in a sack. When he finished gathering up the garden stuff, he said goodbye and limped down the path toward the street.

After we went inside, Livy said she had some schoolwork to do, so I decided to go up to the third floor and practice karate for a while. A good hard workout usually clears my brain, and I needed that. It seemed like ages since I left the farm to get acquainted with my twin sister. It didn't look like I was going to get to know her very fast. She seemed stuck up to me. If Mother was here, she'd tell me to trust in the Lord and He'd take care of everything. I've been wondering about it all day.

Four: First Day of School

Tuesday morning Livy dropped me off at the high school. Seeing all the kids happy and talking to each other like old friends made me feel lonely and left out. So I let out a silent karate yell for courage and threw back my shoulders as if I owned the place. Like my friend that taught me karate always says: "Walk proud as though you're not scared of anything, especially when you are." I was doing my best to walk proud when I heard a girl's voice call my name.

"Seamus, wait for me." I turned around to see Janet Radcliffe getting out of the back seat of the convertible I saw parked in the driveway yesterday. But Shannon and Derek were just sitting in the front seat looking at each other.

I waved back at Janet, feeling glad to see a friendly face. She had her ponytail tied back with a yellow ribbon that matched her blouse. Her brown swing skirt swished around her knees as she hurried across the parking lot. Don't get me wrong, I don't know a lot about girls' clothes, but Livy said these swing skirts are real popular now. Just as Janet got close, the big pile of books she was carrying slipped out of her arms and fell in all directions.

"Here, let me get them," I said, stooping over at the same time she did. Our heads banged together with a dull thud, and we both lost our balance and fell backward. I got up fast and looked at Janet, still sitting there among her books. "Are you hurt?" I asked, and reached down to help her up.

"I'm fine, I think. Boy, you sure have a hard head." She rubbed her forehead a minute, and then I pulled her to her feet. "I think I'll just stand here while you get my books. I don't want to do that again," Janet laughed. By the time we had our books sorted out and were starting across the parking lot, Shannon and Derek came by holding hands. Janet called out to them, "Hey, you guys, wait up. I want you to meet someone." They stopped and looked at me, "This is Seamus Sanford," Janet said. "He's Miss Sanford's brother."

"Oh, hello, Seamus," Shannon said without much enthusiasm. "This is Derek Radcliffe. He's a senior this year." I remembered my manners and offered him my hand. He really put on the pressure. It was his way of telling me quiet-like how tough he was.

"Glad to meet you, Seamus," Derek lifted his eyebrows and grinned at me like he'd just heard a joke. "How'd you meet my sister so fast?"

Before I had a chance to say anything, Janet spoke up. "Miss Sanford introduced us yesterday when I was running. Seamus is really fast. He'll make the track team for sure."

"Come on Derek, I want to get to the gym to see whose homeroom I'm in," Shannon said, putting her hand on his arm. They walked away without saying a word.

"What's with her? She isn't usually rude," Janet said. "She's really been different since her mother was killed in that automobile accident last fall."

We started walking to the front door together. Pretty soon I said, "She's sure got a case on your brother. Livy invited her to lunch yesterday, but she could hardly wait to get out of there. Said she was going to play tennis, but we saw her at the swimming pool with Derek."

"She's been crazy about him forever, but this summer is the first Derek has paid any attention to her," Janet said, shaking her head like she didn't understand what was going on. "Come on, I'll show you where we find our homerooms."

Janet pushed her way through the double front doors into a big hall where the principal's office and several other offices were. A wide stairs led up to the second floor, but Janet led me down a few steps in the opposite direction. We headed toward the gym. There must have been three hundred students trying to see the lists of names posted around the gym walls.

Being six feet tall is handy for looking over folks' heads, so I went to the sophomore section and found my name on Mrs. Lindsey's list. I'd just turned to look for Janet when I heard someone ask, "Say, Stretch, do you see Schaefer on that list?"

I looked down into a face full of freckles with green eyes that gave off sparks of pure devilment. I couldn't help grinning at him. "If the name is Bill, "Scooter" Schaefer, it's right below mine," I said without having to look back at the list. I'd never known anyone named Scooter.

"That's right," he answered. His hair was about the color of a new broom and stood up just as straight. "What's the teacher's name?"

"Lindsey," I answered, and moved back to give others room to see the list.

"Oh, damn!" he said, and his grin disappeared like the sun going behind a cloud. "She was my dad's

English teacher and a real pain in the ass when it came to punctuation. My dad hated her when he was in her class, but when he got to college, he went through English like a breeze."

"Well, I reckon she can't be all bad then," I laughed and stuck out my hand. "My name is Seamus Sanford, and I'm new here."

"Folks usually call me Scooter, for some stupid reason. Come on, I'll show you to her room, the same one she's had for twenty years."

I looked around for Janet and finally saw her talking to Shannon. It looked like they were having a disagreement, so I told Scooter I'd be right back. I tried to make enough noise so they'd hear me, but neither one looked up. Then I heard Janet's angry voice. "He's not a country bumpkin. He's sweet and good-looking. You could at least be polite to him!" She turned around and would have run into me if I hadn't moved fast.

"You weren't going to drop your books again, were you?" I asked Janet. She stood there looking madder and a wet hen for a minute, and then she laughed.

"Oh, Seamus, you surprised me. I was just going to look for you," she said. Her brown eyes sparkled when she smiled at me, and I felt my heart flutter real funny-like. She'd been sticking up for me and thought I was good looking. Nobody but Mother and Livy had ever accused me of that before, and I liked it. I liked it a whole lot. I was so busy thinking about what Janet had said, I barely heard Scooter come up beside me.

"Hi, Janet. Do you know this guy?" Scooter asked her, but he grinned at me like he'd just heard some juicy gossip.

Janet nodded and asked, "Did you just meet?"

"Yeah, and it looks like we'll be in Mrs. Lindsey's English class together," Scooter laughed and jabbed me in the ribs. "I hope you're good at punctuation, Seamus."

"Well, I get by. My sister's a real stickler about it and won't let me get by with a thing."

Scooter looked puzzled for a minute, then Janet spoke up. "Seamus is Miss Sanford's brother. She's the principal at North. Remember I told you about her last year when she substituted until they could find another English teacher."

"Oh, yeah," he laughed and clapped me on the back. "Maybe I'll pass English after all." Just then the bell rang for the first class, and everyone started toward the doors.

Scooter and me got to Mrs. Lindsey's room on the second floor a few minutes before class started, so he headed for the back of the room. I was about to follow him when Mrs. Lindsey spoke to me. "You're Seamus Sanford, aren't you?"

"Yes, ma'am," I answered, trying to think how she'd know who I was. I guess I must of looked surprised because she smiled at me for a minute, then she said my sister had described me when she signed me up for her class. When I looked around the room at the other kids, I knew I stuck out like a sore thumb. I was the only one there with red hair. After I heard what a tough teacher she was, I wasn't surprised Livy had asked to have me in her class. Teachers are like that. They always pick the toughest one for their kids.

"Your sister said I wasn't supposed to let you get by on your good looks." Then she laughed like she thought that was real funny. That's just a joke between Livy and me, but Mrs. Lindsey seemed to understand it. She was a lot nicer than Scooter let on, so I was glad I hadn't paid much attention to him.

When the last bell rang, Mrs. Lindsey said we'd meet here every morning for homeroom the first ten minutes of the hour to get the announcements and take care of any school business before English. She gave us our schedules and talked about the books we needed before she made assignments. She explained that we'd have a short day today to give the teachers a chance to do some last minute scheduling and have a faculty meeting.

It turned out that Scooter was in my geometry and history classes, too, but that wasn't any big surprise since all sophomores have to take those subjects. I found out during the announcements there are thirteen teachers here and three hundred and fifty-seven students. That's three times more than at Toledo. I felt a little worried about how I'd be able to stand up with all these smart town kids.

When I got home at noon I was surprised to see Livy's car parked in the circle drive. She was in the kitchen making sandwiches when I came in. "I didn't know you'd be home for lunch," I said, putting my books on the table.

"I wasn't expecting to, but Judge Williams called me at school to talk about Shannon. He knew you were here, and he said he'd like to meet you. I told him I'd drop you off at his office since you have the afternoon off. After my attempt to help you make friends with Shannon, I think we'd better be careful she doesn't think her Dad's trying to push you at her, too." Livy stopped to take a breath, then went on.

"Now he's worried about her romance with Derek, and I can't blame him."

I didn't know what to say, but I didn't have a good feeling about Derek either. He was so sure of himself, like nothing had ever happened to him he didn't want to happen. He seemed to have a strong hold on my twin sister, and she couldn't stand the sight of me. Maybe I was jealous after hoping so long we'd finally meet and get to be like family.

"Well, I can't say I blame the judge for being worried, not after seeing the way Shannon looks at him like he's a Greek god." Things weren't going the way I'd hoped, that's for sure. "So when does the judge want me to come to his office?"

"He said court would be recessed until two, so I'll drop you by the courthouse on the way back to school if that's okay with you." Livy grinned at me and handed me the sandwich plate. "Here, you'd better have a sandwich before we go," Livy said.

Later, after I'd found my way through the big courtroom to the judge's office, I felt nervous and could hardly talk. If I was at home Dad would ask if the cat had got my tongue. Just thinking about him made me feel better, so I took a deep breath and knocked on the judge's office door.

When it opened I was surprised to see a husky-built man with his shirt sleeves rolled up, standing there in his sock feet. His thick brown hair was sprinkled with gray, and it kind of hung over his forehead like bangs. He wasn't near as old as Dad, but his face looked tired and sad like he hadn't slept good for a long time. He didn't look like Lincoln, but his face had the same kind of sadness.

"Come in, Seamus, I've been looking forward to meeting you." When he smiled, his eyes twinkled and he didn't look so sad. The way he shook my hand made me feel like I was a grown man that he was glad to meet. "Sit down," he said, moving his briefcase full of folders off the chair.

"Are you studying about a case?" I asked since I didn't know what else to say.

"Yes. There's always another one to think about," he said, sitting down behind his cluttered desk. "I've wanted to meet you ever since your sister came here to be the principal at North. She told me about you shortly after my wife's death, and somehow it made me feel better knowing Shannon had a blood relative. Now you're actually going to school here. It all seems like a strange coincidence," he paused, like he was trying to find the right words.

"Yeah," I agreed, wondering how the judge would take to Mother's ideas about why God did things like He did. I thought about it a minute, but he looked so nice and common I decided to tell him. "If Mother was here she'd say the Lord works in mysterious ways." He nodded like he understood, so I went on, "But things aren't working out the way I hoped they would."

"No, I'm sure they aren't. When Olivia told me you were coming, we hoped there would be a common bond between you and Shannon." He folded his hands into a church steeple while he thought. "Oh, she's started to do some of the things she used to, but she isn't fooling me. She's still so angry and hurt that she just hasn't accepted the fact that her mother's gone."

"Well, it hasn't been a year yet. Maybe after more time passes she'll finally begin to understand."

The judge nodded his head and smiled at me. "You're a very perceptive young man, far more mature than most boys your age. I can see why Olivia is proud of you."

I didn't know what to say, so I just nodded and waited for him to go on. "I'm sorry about the way Shannon's treating you, but I guess she must think

Olivia is trying to promote a friendship she doesn't want."

"I know. She's finally got Derek to pay attention to her, and I look just like a dumb kid from the farm," I said, squirming in my chair. "But I wouldn't want her to know I'm her brother until she wouldn't be ashamed of me." I took a big breath and added, "I don't want her to find out now."

"I understand, and I won't say a word. But in Shannon's defense, I want to tell you how close she was to her mother. If it's possible, they were even closer than if they'd been related by blood. When the Orphan Train stopped in Paris twelve years ago, the first baby Sarah saw was Shannon. I guess her red hair just pulled my wife to her. At the same time Sarah saw Shannon, another woman was giving the nun who accompanied the orphans from New York, the number that was pinned on Shannon's dress, but Sarah just grabbed Shannon and said she was hers. The nun tried to get Sarah to let go, but by then, Shannon had her arms around Sarah so tight, they couldn't pry her loose. Finally, the other woman just gave up and took another baby."

"Was I there? Did you see me?"

"No, I didn't go with Sarah, I had court that day, so Suzanne Radcliffe went with her. I don't think

Sarah would have seen you, even if you'd been right in front of her. All she wanted was a little girl, and when she saw one that actually looked like her, that was it." I could see tears welling up in the judge's eyes, but he just blinked them away and swallowed hard. He didn't say anything until he heard a commotion out in the courtroom. Then he looked at his watch and said, "Oh, my. I'd better get my shoes on. I forgot all about court."

He laughed like he was happier than he'd been when I came in, and I was glad. I really liked the judge and wished I could do something to help him. I waited until he had his shoes on, then I got up. He reached for his robe and came around the desk rolling down his sleeves. He smiled and said, "I hope we can get better acquainted. Maybe I can come out and watch you work Regina's horses some day."

We shook hands at the door, and I noticed the courtroom was half full. I felt good that such an important man wanted to talk to me and almost forgot about court. On the way out I wondered if anyone thought I was in trouble with the law. Of course, I didn't know anybody, but it seemed like a lot of people knew me. I guess I do stand out some. Mary Ruth told me last year I reminded her of a flagpole with the top painted red.

That night at supper I told Livy about my visit with the judge, and she listened thoughtful-like, not saying a word until I finished. "Richard Williams is a very sensitive man, and he's had a real load to carry these last months. Not only has he lost his wife, it hurts him to see his daughter so troubled. Now, there's this romance with Derek. He's afraid to say too much to Shannon about Derek when she's only beginning to come back to life. But it couldn't have happened at worse time. She's so vulnerable right now."

I just nodded my head and listened to Livy. She's always talked to me like I understood everything. Most adults talk to kids like they don't have feelings, like they don't feel happy or sad the same as they do. But not Livy.

"I wonder why Derek's mother doesn't talk to him about this. It would be awful if he just decided to drop Shannon." Then I thought of something that could be worse, remembering what Livy had said about Derek being a lady's man. I looked up at Livy, and I could feel my face getting red, just thinking about our sister Rose. She got in the family way and had to get married right out of high school.

"You're thinking about Rose, aren't you?" Livy sighed before going on. "That really hurt Mother.

With five girls, Mother has had her worries. Thank heavens Alvina has been lucky so far." Suddenly Livy grinned. "I guess I shouldn't be talking about things like this with you. But I think it's time adults told young people what to expect about life and sex. It's just stupid to think that if they don't know about it, it won't happen. Some day, schools will offer sex education and save a lot of heartaches."

I'd about decided Livy had finished her sermon, so I got up and started cleaning off the table. I'd had plenty time after I saw the judge to make a double recipe of stew for supper, and I could tell Livy was glad. She didn't say so, but I knew she was tired after the first day of school. I figured I'd be glad there was enough stew left over for supper tomorrow.

I found out the next day that they have cross-country races here in the fall because the football team's using the playing field. At Toledo, we didn't have enough boys for a football team, so we had track in the fall. The coach explained this to me today because he's also my geometry teacher. After he finished making his assignments, he asked the boys to sign up for the team.

The Red Headed Girl

Five: The Dance

The first week was over before I knew it, and I'd settled into my new routine real easy. Early in the morning, I do karate before I tend the horses. Then I go to school to practice typing. I've almost learned the keyboard, but my long fingers seem to trip over themselves sometimes. Miss Greathouse says I'm doing better than she expected, but I reckon she wasn't expecting much. Now that I'm getting the hang of it, I can see that typing and playing the guitar are sort of alike. If I get my fingers on the right keys to start with, things work out just fine.

Spanish isn't as bad as I thought either. I keep memorizing vocabulary words and go around practicing 'em under my breath. The horses seem to like to hear me conjugate verbs out loud when I feed and water them, but I don't have time to ride much. After school I try to get in an hour of running before heading home. I want to get practiced up for the cross-country meet next week.

I've been running ever since we moved down to the Bend farm where it was two miles to school. But I have to admit I started running because I didn't like Buster Johnson's company. Buster was the school bully until I threw him in the ditch after he hit Mary Ruth with a rock. I'd been learning karate from Pete Gaines for a while, but I wasn't very good at the time. I guess I just did what Pete taught me without thinking when Buster grabbed me by the hair. I hate to have my hair pulled worse than anything. It's thick and curly and Buster had a real good hold on it. I reckon I was lucky he thought being dumped in the muddy ditch once was enough to leave me alone.

Mother seemed to think it was the good Lord that gave me the strength to defend myself, but it's like Pete said: "Son, you need more than prayers to stop a bully." To tell you the truth, I never did understand that business in the Bible about turning the other cheek.

Well, anyway, I was peeling potatoes for supper Thursday night when Livy came home with a bundle under her arm. She was looking real proud of herself when she pecked me on the cheek and started unwrapping the package. "Guess what I have here?" She didn't wait for me to guess. She just opened it and pulled out a pair of navy blue slacks. "Notice they're the latest style with double pleats and 22-inch bottoms."

"But, Livy, what do I need them for? I already have a pair of Sunday pants."

"Those old things," she said. "Why, they're too short and besides, they're out of style. There was a good-looking suit at Hedges for $18.95, but these slacks for $3.49 were more in my price range." When Livy held them up to her waist, the cuffs drug on the floor. "You'll look so handsome tomorrow night when you take me to the Freshman Frolic."

"But I'm not a freshman."

"No, but I was the eighth grade class sponsor last year, and they sent me a special invitation. I'm taking you as my escort, little brother. I haven't been to a dance in ages, and I don't care if it's only a record dance in the gym. What do you say, Fred?" Sometimes Livy calls me Fred Astaire to tease me.

I put the crock of potatoes on the table and swung Livy around a few times before I answered her. "Why, I'd be proud to take you to the dance, Miss Sanford." I guess Duke heard us laughing, and thought something was wrong, so he started barking at the back door. Poor dog wants attention so much, he's even made up to Stormy. She walks around the back yard with him, rubbing up against him as if she likes him. There's just no accounting for cats' attitudes.

After supper Livy wanted me to practice the new dance lesson she got in the mail that week. She's taking a correspondence course, and the company sends a record along with instructions on how to do the step. They even have a pattern to put on the floor so you'll know exactly where to put your feet. Once a month, Livy goes over to the dance studio in Terre Haute, Indiana, fifteen miles away. She gets to practice with an instructor to see if she's learned the steps right.

Livy's been teaching me to do ballroom dancing since I was knee high to a grasshopper, and she says I have natural rhythm. My friend Pete that taught me karate was a dancer in vaudeville when he was young, and he showed me how to do a lot of different dances like the Smoky Mountain Buck Dance, the Highland fling and an Irish jig. I don't know about having natural rhythm, but when I hear music, I feel it in my feet.

The next morning before English class, Scooter told me all about what to expect at the dance that night because he went to it last year. He's one of the shortest boys in the sophomore class, and he hates to dance with girls taller than him. Since he didn't want to miss the dances, he decided to go into the disk jockey business. He already had a good collection of records and a portable record player, so when a class wants to have a dance, they pay him to play records. He even plays special songs if they tell him ahead of time.

When Livy and me got to the high school gym Friday night, the dance had already started. Scooter was on the stage behind a long table where he had his record player set up and his records arranged the way he planned to play 'em. He even had a tablecloth with his name in felt letters hanging down across the front, and he looked like the announcer on Lucky Strike Hit Parade. I got a picture by sending in the wrappers of two packs of Lucky Strike cigarettes to WGN in Chicago. Naturally I didn't buy the cigarettes, I found the wrappers in the trashcan in the boys' locker room last year. I didn't tell Mother I'd done it, because she thinks smoking is a terrible sin right next to drinking.

"Now," Scooter said in his announcer's voice, "here's that old favorite from 1938, 'Falling in Love with Love.' So, girls, drag them boys off the bleachers and let's dance." Livy didn't even lay her purse down, she just put her arm on my shoulder, and we started twirling across the dance floor. We've worked up a pretty good routine for the fox trot. After we twirl a few times, we do the walk-away four steps before we go back into the two-step. Since I'd never danced in public with Livy, I didn't know how we looked, but everyone kind of got out of the way when we danced by. Some couples just stopped and watched, so I guess all that practice paid off.

When the song was over, Scooter came back to the microphone and started talking about Fred Astaire and Rita Hayworth just dropping by, and everyone clapped. Naturally, the freshmen liked Livy a lot, but they didn't know me. "Just kidding, you guys. This is your own Miss Sanford and her little brother, Seamus. He's a sophomore here at Marshall High this year. Now, let's liven things up with a fast one. Here's 'Chattanooga Choo-choo.'"

After dancing another time or two, Livy told me it was time for me to ask some of the girls to dance. Since I didn't see anyone I knew, I asked my English teacher, Mrs. Lindsey. I was glad Scooter put on "I'll Never Smile Again" because it's easy to dance to. I didn't need to worry; Mrs. Lindsey was light on her feet and followed me just fine for being so old. She must be forty at least. I noticed that Livy made one of the boys get up and dance with her, but he didn't act too mad about it.

When I walked Mrs. Lindsey back to her chair, I was surprised to see Janet and Shannon had just come in with the judge. They were looking around the room for some of their friends, and the judge was shaking hands with the principal, Mr. Wallace. I was surprised to see the judge, but I supposed parents got invited to chaperone, too.

He was all dressed up, but he still looked sad when he took Shannon's hand and led her out on the floor. Janet smiled at me, and I didn't even have to ask her to dance. She gave me her hand and we slid out on the floor as smooth as you please. She's about as tall as Livy, so I felt real comfortable dancing with her. She just leaned against me and followed real well. I felt my heart thumping through my sweater, but I didn't know what to make of it. I guess Janet must of felt the same way because she looked up at me, her eyes smiling like she was happy. "You're sure a good dancer, Seamus."

"I've never danced much with anyone but Livy, but I reckon we're doing okay."

Scooter was playing a new song that had just come out, and we were doing the jitterbug to "Deep in the Heart of Texas." It's that song where the singer pauses and everyone stops dancing and claps their hands a few times before the singer starts up again. It's a good song, but it's hard to remember where you left off dancing.

Ever since we got there, I noticed two boys sitting on the bleachers watching every move I made.

I'd seen 'em in the restroom smoking a few times. Of course, it's strictly against the rules, but they always stand by the windows with their cigarettes hanging outside so they can drop 'em in case a teacher comes in. One boy's hair is dark and wavy, and he wears it longer than the rest of us. His skin is dark like he has a real heavy suntan. The other boy's built like a wrestler and I heard him call the dark one Farris.

A minute after Scooter put on another slow tune; Farris came over and kind of shoved me back to cut in on me. Janet didn't look very happy about it, but since I didn't want to cause trouble, I stepped away. Farris grinned at Janet and pulled her close to him and twirled her away. It was plain to me he was showing off. It wasn't long until the principal walked out on the floor and tapped Farris on the shoulder and motioned for him to give Janet some room. Before long, Farris had another death grip on her, so I cut in. She looked relieved, but if looks could kill, I'd of keeled over dead right there. Just before he stomped off, he said under his breath, "You'll be sorry, you bastard."

I've been called that before, and I didn't like it any better now than I did the first time. It put a damper on the good time I was having, and I guess it didn't make Janet too happy either. So after the song was over, we decided to sit down for a while. I was just as glad we had because that was when the judge asked Livy to dance. Scooter put on "Begin the Beguine," a tune with a Latin beat. I could see the kids trying to figure out what step to do to the music, so most of them just stood still and watched Livy and the judge.

Somehow, the day I met the judge sitting there without his shoes on, I hadn't thought about him being a fancy dancer. It really surprised me when he started leading Livy into the very step I'd just learned. Livy was as light as a feather on her feet, and he led her around the floor real smooth-like. As they danced, his sad face lightened up and he seemed to get younger. When he did the fancy dips and twirls, Livy didn't miss a beat, and I could tell she was having a good time.

Suddenly, I could feel eyes staring at me from behind. Then from a few steps above me I heard a voice say, "Look at our prissy Miss Sanford out there shaking her hips at the judge. I bet she's a hot piece in bed." I didn't even have to turn around to know who'd said it.

Before I knew what I was doing, I'd moved up behind Farris and took hold of his elbow in a vice grip. Then I leaned close to his ear so he couldn't help hearing me, "If I ever hear talk like that about my sister, I'll know where it started. No matter where you hide, I'll find you and scour your plow good. Do you understand?" When I was sure he understood, I went back to my seat.

I didn't say anything to Janet, but she'd seen me giving Farris an ear full. It wasn't long before they headed for the door, so Janet started telling me what she knew about 'em. "I don't know what you did to Nelson Farris, but I wouldn't turn my back to him from now on. He and Bert Garwood were in trouble all the time last year. They got paddled for cheating in math, and then Miss Sanford made them sand all the desks in our classroom for scratching dirty words on them. He's a pain, but I feel real sorry for Nelson's mom," Janet stopped talking for a minute, then she added, "because she isn't married."

"You mean he's, uh, that is...." I stumbled around trying to find the right word. "You mean he's illegitimate?"

Janet nodded. "I've heard that his father is one of the gypsies that comes through here every year. They camp on the Farris farm. Mother said Nelson's mom was kind of a loner in high school, and, well, some of those men are good looking." Janet's voice kind of trailed off and stopped for a minute.

"Nelson's mom works in the shoe factory in Terre Haute, and they live with her folks on the farm."

"What about the other one, Bert Garwood?"

"I don't know much about him. He just moved here last year. I think his folks got a divorce and left him with his grandparents. I guess they can't do much with him."

While we'd been talking, some of the mothers had brought in punch and cookies, and everyone crowded around the refreshment table as soon as Scooter announced intermission.

Saturday morning I was giving the stable a good cleaning when Livy came out to tell me the judge was coming over to go riding with me. I was real pleased about that, so I worked a little faster to get the stable cleaned before he got here. By the time Livy brought the judge to the fence, I'd finished putting down clean straw for the horses and was giving them a good brushing. He was wearing brown jodhpurs and riding boots and looking real chipper.

"Good morning, Seamus. I hope you have time to go riding with me. I haven't been on a horse since...." His face kind of fell, and I knew he was thinking about his dead wife. Finally he finished, "not since last October."

"Morning, sir," I said. "The horses will be glad for a good workout. I'll saddle 'em up as soon as I finish here." I was feeling a little uneasy since I was wearing old overalls and four-buckle overshoes for cleaning out the straw. "Then I'll go change clothes."

Livy had climbed up on the top rail of the wood fence to watch me work. She was wearing a pair of dungarees rolled up to the knees and a blue striped shirt that made her eyes look even bluer than ever. Without her dress-up clothes and makeup, she looked like a school- girl. I noticed the judge was watching her out of the corner of his eye, and he was smiling. When I went to put the grooming things away and brought out the saddles, the judge said he'd saddle up while I changed. I didn't argue because I was glad to get away.

When I got back, the judge and Livy were holding the horses out on the driveway, laughing about something. We both mounted up, and Livy waved as we rode away. We took our time going down Second Street to the fairground, but when we got on the racetrack, we let the horses go. It was a nice smooth track, and the horses seemed to feel the excitement running along together.

I'd always wondered how a jockey felt racing around the track at the Cumberland County fair, and it was even better than I imagined. I was riding Star, and she seemed to skim above the dirt, like Pegasus flying through the air. All I had to do was lean down low and hold the reins. I forgot all about the judge and Blaze, but after the second time around, I thought I'd better slow Star down and give her a breather.

The judge and Blaze came galloping up next to us a few seconds later, and I looked up to see Jimmy Black leaning on the fence grinning. He was clapping like he'd won a bet on Star.

"Hi, Jimmy," I said. "This is Judge Williams." The judge got off the horse and shook hands with Jimmy.

"How are you, Jimmy? I haven't seen you for a while," the judge smiled like he really was glad to see Jimmy.

"Oh, I'm fair to middlin'," but seein' you two riding around, I remember how good my racin' days was," Jimmy grinned back at the judge. Then he looked at me. "You've got a light hand with horses, son. How'd you like riding on a real track?"

"Just fine. And Star liked it, too," I said, leaning down to pat her head. "I think we'd better walk them a little to cool off," I said to Jimmy.

"Good thinking. They haven't been rode since the Ashley's went to Washington. Next time you come over, stop by my place an' wet your whistle." Then Jimmy said goodbye and limped back around the grandstand out of sight.

The judge got back on Blaze and we started around the track. We didn't say much for a while, just enjoying the sunshine and the feel of good horses under us.

Finally, I asked, "Did Shannon know you were coming over to ride with me?"

"No, she has ballet lessons over at Terre Haute on Saturday mornings, so she and Janet went over on the Turner Bus." Livy told me that the Turners have a little company that makes it real handy for folks to get to Terre Haute and some other towns around here.

We didn't talk much, so I reckon the judge had as much on his mind as I did. After a while he asked me, "Did you have a good time at the dance last night?" I nodded and he went on talking. "I noticed you're quite a dancer. Where'd you learn to dance like that?"

"Livy. She loves to dance."

"Looks like you enjoy it, too," he laughed. "I liked the way you cut in on that Farris boy. I didn't think much of the way he was dancing with Janet."

"Me either," I admitted. I guess I must have said it pretty sharp because the judge looked up in surprise. I'd been wondering if I should tell him what Farris said about Livy shaking her hips at him. I knew I wasn't going to tell Livy and worry her, so I just started out and told him everything.

"Well, no wonder you're put out with the Farris boy. This is a small town, and people do talk. I had no idea one dance would start gossip." The judge looked at me for a minute, then he went on. "That boy's had it rough. Everyone knows he doesn't have a father, and I'm sure he's heard enough said about that. I'd like to do something to help him, but he has a real chip on his shoulder. At the same time, we can't let him spread nasty gossip about Olivia."

I nodded as the judge talked. Even though he's an important man, he's real comfortable to be with. So, I decided to tell him what I'd said to Farris. "I've been thinking about this, and I figure he didn't like me because I was dancing with Janet. And Janet said Livy made him sand desks last year, so he's probably still mad at her."

The judge looked at me kinda funny-like, then he laughed. "You're quite the psychologist, Seamus. That all sounds logical, and I don't doubt it's right. In most gossip, there's usually a grain of truth. I was having a good time for the first time in months. And those Latin beats do make the dancers look a little provocative.

We rode on for a while, and I felt better after talking to him. This was something I couldn't talk to Dad about, but just thinking about him made me a little homesick. "I reckon so," I said, "and Livy is a mighty good dancer. I don't want to worry her about this."

"But if you do have any trouble with the boy or he does start talking out of turn, be sure to call me at the office. I wouldn't like Shannon to hear of it. Her mother's death is still too fresh for her to think of another woman in my life."

By now, we were at the fairground gates, so we headed back down Second Street for the stable.

Six: My Father's in the Movies

October's always been my favorite month with warm days and cool nights. I love the colors of fall when leaves turn gold and red. I don't even mind when they start to fall and remind me that winter's on the way.

Maybe it isn't just the warm colors; maybe it's the smells of fall coming from Mother's kitchen when she cooks for corn shuckers. That's when cousin Lloyd stays at our house a few weeks while he helps Dad with the corn harvest.

Yeah, I miss being at home at this time of the year. But, Livy needs me, and I'm happy to be here in Marshall. I write Mother a postcard every week to let her know I'm okay and she writes back.

That's how I found the old recipe this afternoon that somehow fell out of Mrs. Ashley's desk. I couldn't figure out where the recipe came from, but the desk's one of those Chippendales that has a lot of drawers in the front. You pull them out with fancy curly-ques that look like they're part of the decoration until you find out they're handles for the drawers. I thought I'd inspected every drawer when I put my things in the desk, but I reckon I didn't.

I don't know where the recipe came from, but it was yellow with age and brown spots sprinkled across like something had been spilled on it. At the top of the card was a name. Abigail Archer. I wondered if she'd hid it there or if it just got stuck somehow. After I'd studied the recipe I decided I'd try it and surprise Livy at supper.

I knew we had everything I'd need to stir it up. Ozark Pudding, that's the name of the recipe, and besides it looked easy enough for me. I took my Spanish book along to the kitchen and set it up on the counter so I could memorize my vocabulary while I worked. Stormy must of heard me, 'cause she started climbing on the screen door wanting in. Then Duke began whining something pitiful, so I shut the doors to the dining room and to Mrs. Ashley's office and let 'em in. Old Duke went over to his basket and started chewing on a bone, and Stormy begged for a saucer of milk. They don't get much attention these days with all I have to do, so I didn't mind.

It didn't take any time to beat the egg with 3/4 cup of sugar, 3 tablespoons of flour, a pinch of salt and 1/4 teaspoon of baking powder. Then I chopped up an apple and a 1/2-cup of nuts and stirred 'em in. I poured it all in a greased pan and stuck it in the oven for thirty minutes. By the time I'd finished my Spanish homework and recited the vocabulary for Stormy a few times, the Ozark Pudding was done. It had puffed up nice and golden and smelled even better than it looked. So I cut me a bite before peeling the potatoes.

It's cool enough these evenings to enjoy soup, and we had a loaf of Mother's bread to eat with it. She always sends something home with us from the farm, and her bread and butter are real special now that I've been eating them store-bought.

By the time I had supper ready, I could hear Livy's car coming down the driveway. I knew she'd be tired because she had to stay late at school to get her agenda ready for the school board meeting. This being the first Monday of October, it was the regular meeting night. Livy dreads these meetings because there's always trouble from old man Sinclair when she brings up the need for school supplies.

He's never been married and thinks women have no place in school administration, or any other place for that matter. Livy says he's meaner than cat shit, and she hardly ever talks like that. She thinks the only way he could have got that ornery is that he suffers from chronic constipation. Only, now it's spread to his brain so he can't think straight. She doesn't understand how he can talk so much and say so little when he's trying to explain why she can't have the money she needs for school supplies. She just can't figure out how he can suffer from constipation of the brain and diarrhea of the mouth at the same time.

Well, maybe that's not exactly the way she said it, but I think that's what she meant.

"What's that wonderful smell?" Livy called out when she stepped up on the back porch. Duke and Stormy had been curled up asleep, and both sprung up when they heard her voice.

"Come 'n see," I said, feeling mighty proud of myself.

"Oh, Shamie, you've made a dessert! What's the occasion?" Livy dropped her purse and satchel on the chair by the door.

I was so excited, I just started telling her about finding the recipe. "I think there's a secret compartment in that desk. Look what I found," I said, handing her the recipe. "Be careful, it's real brittle."

"Why, look at that name, Abigail Archer. She's Regina's grandmother. How did you find it?"

"I started to write a postcard to mother, but I forgot which drawer I put it in. So I had to pull out several before I found the cards. When I started putting things back, I noticed the recipe there with the cards."

"How exciting," Livy said, cutting a bite of dessert with the knife I'd left next to the pan. "Um-m, that's good. I'm starved." She washed her hands at the sink and then walked over to the stove to stir the soup.

"Sit down," I told her, "and I'll bring your soup. You slice the bread." We didn't talk much while we ate, but when we'd finished our first bowl, Livy got up to get more.

"So how was your cross-country practice? Did you make better time today?"

"Yeah, a little. Coach says I'm gaining on Willie Scott, and he's a senior. I know all the turns around the course through the fairgrounds now and don't need to slow down much. But I don't know how I'll do when we go to Casey to the four-way meet this week."

"Oh, you'll do fine. Just remember, you're really competing against yourself. Don't be discouraged if you don't finish among the first ones. You're only fourteen." Livy gave me my soup and dipped another one for herself.

When it was time for dessert, she went to the stove and shook the coffee pot to see if any of the morning coffee was left. "It looks like there's just enough for one cup, and I'm the one who has to stay awake at the meeting tonight," Livy grinned at me, put the pot on the front burner, and turned on the gas. While she waited for it to heat, she cut two pieces of Ozark Pudding and put them on dessert plates.

Livy looked at the old recipe as she ate. "Why don't you write to Regina and send her a copy of this?"

"Why, sure, and I'll make one for Mother, too." I wondered why it was called a pudding because it was more like a soft cookie, but it went down real easy. I decided to have another little piece with a glass of milk. After we finished, Livy had to hurry to get to the school board meeting, so I turned on the radio and listened to the "Lone Ranger" while I did the dishes.

I'd just settled down at my desk to do some typing when the telephone rang. It was Scooter Schaefer.

"Hi, Seamus. What are you doing?" Scooter wanted to know.

"Typing a copy of the old recipe I found in Mrs. Ashley's desk," I said.

"No kidding! What for?"

"I'm going to send it to Mrs. Ashley. It has her grandmother's name on it."

"You mean Abigail Archer? Did you know that her husband helped found this town?"

"Yeah, Livy told me about the colonel. He'd be an interesting man to write about for our history report," I said.

"Yeah, he would. I might write about Joseph Duncan. He was the sixth governor of Illinois. Maybe we could work on it together." I thought that was interesting, but I'd had an idea about writing a report on Lincoln in Marshall.

"Say, Scooter, have you ever heard any stories about Lincoln here in Marshall?" I figured since Scooter knew so much about local history he might know some stories about Lincoln.

"Just one. Back in 1850 he defended a man accused of manslaughter. William Davis was his name. He was convicted and sentenced to the penitentiary for three years."

"Was that all there was to the case?" I asked.

"No, Lincoln thought the sentence was too long. So he wrote to the governor of Illinois two years later and asked him to pardon Davis. But the governor wouldn't do it."

"How come?" I asked.

"Hey, what do you expect? I'm no talking history book. Look it up yourself." I could tell Scooter had something else on his mind because I could almost hear his brain click to a different subject. "Say," Scooter asked, "what did you do to make Nelson Farris so mad at you? He was really bad-mouthing you at Radamaker's Ice Cream Store today."

"I don't know, but I think he has a crush on Janet. Did you see him cut in on me at the freshman dance?"

"Yeah, I did. He's been trying to get her to pay attention to him a long time, but she can't stand him. Well, if I was you, I'd watch out for him."

"Thanks for the warning. I never have time to hang around after school. That's when I run."

"I've seen you. You're a running fool. It looks boring to me, but I see you've been placing pretty good with the rest of the team."

"I guess I'm doing okay. But it's not boring. I do a lot of thinking while I run. Of course running makes me stiff and sore, but I like it anyway."

"I'll come out and watch the next time you have a meet here. I hear you finish in front of the grandstand at the fairground."

"Yeah, we start from the school and run across that field between 5th and 2nd streets over to the fairground. Then about two miles later we finish back in front of the grandstand."

"That'd be too much territory for my short legs to cover." Scooter stopped talking for a minute before he went on. "Well, I'd better get on my homework. Dad says if I don't start making better grades, he's going to stop my allowance. Puny as it is, I need that money to buy records. You know they cost thirty-five cents apiece."

"Yeah, I know. But don't you do anything to earn the money? Surely your dad wouldn't just give it to you."

"Well, I sweep out and sort the type Dad's always dropping. You know, stuff like that. A print shop's a dirty place. Ink's everywhere."

Late Thursday afternoon when we got back to school from the Casey cross-country meet, Livy was parked in front waiting for me. Coach Sanders and Mr. Wallace, the principal, and another teacher drove us over there in their cars. We'd made a pretty good showing, and I'd come in seventh. That doesn't sound like much, but with four schools at the meet, there were at least fifty runners. I was sure happy to see Livy because I was really tired.

I jumped out of the car and Livy gave me a big hug like she didn't care how sweaty I was. When the guys saw Livy put her arms around me, they all clapped. Willie Scott, the best runner on the team, laughed and called out, "Don't tell me she's your mother, Seamus!"

"I won't," I yelled back. Willie loves to tease me and see my face get red. "See you tomorrow," I said, then I threw my clothes satchel in the car and climbed in.

Livy shifted into low, and we took off for home. When we got there, she told me to go jump in the bathtub and soak in Epson salts to ease my muscles. "We're going down town to the Candy Kitchen for supper."

"How come?" I called back over my shoulder as I headed up the back stairs.

"I got paid today," Livy answered. "Go soak your body, and don't forget the salts."

When I came down a while later, I yelled to Livy that I was going out to tend the horses, and she answered me from the library, where she has a desk. It didn't take me long to pump fresh water and put alfalfa in their mangers inside the stalls. Since the horses don't do much but eat grass all day, I just gave 'em enough to hurry 'em in. I hadn't had anything to eat since lunch, so I was starved.

When we got to the Candy Kitchen, hardly anyone was there. It was too late for the supper trade, and too early for folks to be out of the movie at the Pythian Theater down the street. We found a booth along the wall, and Edna came over to take our order. "How are you, Miss Sanford?" Edna asked Livy. Then she looked at me and said; "I haven't seen you in here since the first week of school." She handed us menus and smiled real friendly-like. Scooter told me she'd been a waitress here for ages and that she was a real good friend to the kids that hung around here.

"I've been busy with school and cross-country." I looked at the menu, but I already knew what I wanted. "I'll take a chocolate milkshake and two toasted cheese sandwiches," I said.

"And I'll have a cup of coffee and a spiced ham sandwich," Livy added, giving Edna back the menu.

"And one big order of French fries for us both, please."

While we waited for our food, Livy told me about the letter she'd gotten from Alvina. She's the youngest girl in the family, five years older than me. She doesn't give me as much trouble as she used to, but she liked to make my life miserable when I was young. Now that she's graduated from high school, she's working in Chicago and living with our sister Rose and her husband.

"You won't believe it, Shamie, Alvina has joined the WAVES, and she's stationed at the Great Lakes Naval Training Station north of Chicago. She said she wanted to be where the men were, and there should be enough at that station," Livy laughed. "Besides, she says of all the women's branches of the service, the WAVES have the best looking uniforms."

"That sounds like Alvina, all right. Does Mother know yet?"

"I don't think so. I expect she wants me to tell her, but she should have had the courtesy to tell the folks about joining before she actually did. She's nineteen and old enough to join even if they didn't want her to."

"She doesn't care whose feelings she hurts as long as she gets what she wants," I said. I hoped I didn't sound as spiteful as I felt. But I couldn't forget all those times Alvina told me if I didn't do what she wanted, she'd see that I got sent back to the orphanage. She even showed me my indenture papers about being sent back until the age of twelve. She found the papers a long time ago when she was snooping in Mother's bureau drawers.

"No, she doesn't," Livy said, her blue eyes had turned shiny and sad. "I know she made your life miserable for a long time."

"Well, I'm a lot bigger than she is now." I didn't finish because our food came. I set to, forgetting all about Alvina. Well, almost.

After we finished eating, we walked down the street and looked into some of the store windows. We stopped to look at the display of men's shoes in the Grabenhumer shoe store. Livy told me she thought I ought to buy a new pair of Sunday shoes when Mrs. Ashley sent my next check. I knew my old ones looked pretty bad, but I had my eyes on a pair of good tennis shoes to run in. We crossed the street at Archer Avenue and Seventh and looked in some more windows.

When we got to the Pythian Theater, we stopped to read the advertisement for the new Gene Autry western. It was "Riding On a Rainbow" with

Smiley Burnett and Mary Lee. Gene Autry's been one of my favorite western singers since he was on the "Barn Dance" at WLS radio station in Chicago. I know most of his songs and can play 'em on my guitar. He's a lot better at singing than he is at acting, but I like his movies even though they sometimes have airplanes and stagecoaches in the same one.

After Mary Lee's name there was an "also featuring" notice of a new singing cowboy named Michael Ryan. It didn't show his picture, but that name made me stop and wonder where I'd seen it before. When I remembered, my breath came in short gasps, and I took hold of Livy's arm.

She looked up at me, worried-like, "What is it, Shamie. Are you okay?"

"You see that name? Michael Ryan? Could that be my father?"

"Why, I wouldn't think so."

"Remember that letter the sisters at the New York Orphan Asylum sent us? It was the letter he wrote my mother about getting a divorce in Nevada? He signed his name Michael, and on my birth certificate, my last name was Ryan, not St. Clair like my mother's. He said he was making a movie. Do you suppose it's him?"

"But that was four years ago. How could we be sure?

"I think I'd know if I saw him. I'd just like to know what he looks like. I never saw a picture of either one of them."

"Oh, Shamie, I understand. But do you think it's a good idea?"

"Maybe I'd feel better about him if I saw him. He might not be as bad as I think."

"I remember how bad you felt that day you read the letter he wrote to your mother when she was expecting you. He told her the reason he left her was because she wouldn't get rid of you." I swallowed hard because I couldn't say anything. Livy nodded her head and said, "Well, if you're sure. We've already missed the newsreel and the serial, but the main film should be starting soon. You sure it isn't going to upset you?"

"No, I want to see if it's him. I want to know."

Livy didn't say any more, she just walked up to the box office and bought the tickets for thirty-five cents apiece.

The Bugs Bunny cartoon was just over when we sat down, so we got to see Gene Autry come riding his horse Champion down the trail singing

"I'm Back in the Saddle Again." Mary Lee's name flashed on the screen followed by Smiley Burnett's, then Gene rode off a-yodeling.

This movie was about like all the rest with Gene and the ranch hands trying to find the bad guys and bring 'em to justice. When Gene and the boys stopped at night, they nearly always did some singing around the campfire. But I could never figure out where the guitars came from because they didn't have 'em tied to their saddles when they rode off.

I was so nervous waiting to see someone that looked like my father, I almost missed him. The camera slowly came to a stop on a man singing on the deck of a steamboat, and my eyes froze. He was a tall, slender man with dark curly hair. The camera rested on his face while he sang to a woman wearing a fancy dress. He looked a lot older than me, but if I didn't know better, I'd of thought it was me standing there.

Suddenly I heard Livy make a funny noise in her throat, and she grabbed hold of my arm and whispered, "You look just like that man, Shamie. If the picture was only in color so we could see what color his hair is." She didn't say any more but sat there holding on to my arm like I was going to be carried off by the characters on the screen. We didn't talk any more 'til the show was over and the audience started to leave. I didn't know about Livy, but my knees were too weak to move, so we waited until everyone else was gone before we got up.

The Red Headed Girl

Seven: Buster's Letter

I look forward to weekends when I have time to get caught up with all my chores. Mrs. Ashley pays me twenty-five cents an hour, so I keep careful track of my time. I usually put in an hour or so a day through the week and ten or twelve on the weekend. Last month I made $16. That's more money than I'd earned at one time in my life.

On Saturdays I have plenty of time to groom the horses and give 'em a good workout on the fairground track. Usually, when the judge isn't busy he rides with me. He says riding horses helps clear the cobwebs from his mind. Besides, I think he likes me as much as I do him. He said since I was Shannon's brother, that kind of made me his son. I liked that a whole lot.

So after I saw my real father in Gene Autry's movie, I told the judge all about it. I even told him about the letter my father wrote to my mother. I could recite it from memory since I'd read it so many times. I had to admit I hated to think I was a bastard back then like Buster said I was.

"It really made me feel bad until I read that letter and found out my mother wanted to keep her own name when she got married. I guess it was because it was her stage name, but she gave me and Shannon his name."

"But you'd rather have had her name, wouldn't you?" the judge asked.

"I reckon so, but it doesn't matter now that I'm adopted."

"Would you like to meet your father, Seamus?"

"I don't think so, but I'd like to know if he's as selfish as he was back when me and Shannon were born. You know, not wanting us and getting a divorce without talking it over with my mother."

"How was he as an actor and singer? Are you glad you saw him?"

"Yeah, I'd always wondered what he looked like. He's a pretty good singer, and Livy says I look just like him. But I think Shannon must look more like our mother."

"Probably, but you two look quite a bit alike. I'm surprised someone hasn't noticed it." I guess I must of looked sad or something because he smiled at me and went on talking. "Don't worry, Seamus, when the time is right, Shannon will come to care for you, and she'll be glad she has a brother. Then you can tell her everything."

"I hope so. Ever since I heard about Shannon I've looked forward to having a real sister, so I reckon I'm disappointed she doesn't even like me. She says we don't have anything in common."

"I'm sure you do, but you've been raised differently. My wife treated Shannon like she was a princess, and she's always had everything she wanted. She grew up hearing classical music, and she's been taking ballet since she was seven. When you see her dance, you'll be impressed with her talent.

"I'd sure like to, but I don't know anything about ballet."

"Well, you'll get a chance to see her next Saturday at Janet's party. Derek's planning a surprise talent show for her, and Scooter's helping him. Shannon's going to perform a number from Cinderella."

"Scooter asked me to sing and play my guitar, but I'm pretty sure she won't like western music." I was feeling mighty low, but the judge laughed and said he sure liked it. That made me feel better because I figured if a man like the judge enjoyed it, it was okay for me, too. When we got home the judge hurried off to an important draft board meeting, so I started practicing the song for Janet's party. I'd decided to do Gene Autry's new song called "South of the Border." If I could get Mr. Vadas to help, I'd like to learn the chorus in Spanish. So I started singing while I brushed the horses.

"South of the border, down Mexico way.

That's where I fell in love, when stars above come out to play.

And now as I wander, my thoughts ever stray,

South of the border down Mexico way.

Hi yi, yi, yi...hi yi, yi, yi."

Old Duke and Stormy had come out to the stables after the judge left, and I think Duke really liked the song, especially the hi, yi, yi, yi part. That's when he started howling like he was singing along. Stormy wasn't much impressed though. She just climbed up in the manger and went to sleep. After I finished brushing the horses and turned them out to pasture, I went inside to have lunch with Livy.

"Who do you know in Hawaii?" Livy asked me when I sat down at the table.

"Nobody," I said, "Why'd you ask?"

"This came in the mail today," Livy handed me a letter. "The handwriting looks like a second grader's."

I didn't recognize the writing, but I did the name, Seaman 2/c Buster Johnson, Fleet Post Office, San Francisco, California. I couldn't figure out what Buster was doing in the navy, so I ripped open the envelope to see.

Dear Seamus

    I reckon you're surprized to hear from me since we didn't see eye to eye at school. Well, I got tard workin in that stinkin garage over in Greenup, so I joined the navy three months ago. It aint as much fun as I thought, but its ok when I work on the big engines of the ship. The reson I'm writin is because in boot camp they had the orneriest son of a bitch I ever laid eyes on in charge of us recruits. He picked on me something awful an I didn't do nothin to him. After I got here at Pearl Harbor and started gettin treated better, I thought about how mean I wuz to you. I never had much luck in school, and you wuz so smart you pissed me off. Well, I'm sorry I was so ornery. I'm lonesome as hell. If you'd write me a letter, I'd like it a lot on account of nobody writes me but ma.

        yore frind,

        Buster

After I finished reading Buster's letter, I gave it to Livy. When she finished, she put it on the table and smiled. "Well, can you beat that! Buster is lonely as hell. Does that make you feel good?"

"Not really. I'm kind of sorry for Buster. After I got over being scared, I started watching him. He was lonesome then, too. Nobody liked him but Russell, and I doubt if he really did. I reckon I'll write to him if it'll make him feel better."

"You don't have a mean bone in your body, Shamie. Mother'd be proud!"

"Do you suppose this is what the verse meant about turning the other cheek? I couldn't do it when Buster was threatening to beat me up all the time, but now that he's clear over in Pearl Harbor, it isn't so hard."

Livy just laughed and started ladling up the soup, "Well, let's eat. I made some vegetable soup this morning while you were doing your chores."

That night at supper we turned on the radio to listen to the news. We wanted to know what was going on, but it was pretty depressing. Each program seemed to start out with stories about the war in

Europe and whether the United States would get into it.

Just last month President Roosevelt told the navy to "shoot on sight any hostile craft attacking American ships or any ships under American escort." This was after an incident in the Atlantic between a German submarine and the destroyer U.S.S. Greer.

Now, the U.S.S. Kearny has been attacked by a German submarine, the President told us, "We Americans have cleared our decks and taken our battle stations."

With all this talk about war, I started thinking about Buster over there in Hawaii, so I said to Livy, "You reckon Buster knows about all this?"

"I don't suppose he could help it, but he's over on the other side of the world. I don't imagine there are any German submarines over there," Livy said, getting up to stack the dishes. "That's enough bad news for tonight. Let's get these dishes done before the Hit Parade comes on. What do think will be number one?"

I had to grin at Livy. She always knows when I'm worried and tries to get my mind on something else. I decided she was right since I couldn't do much about the war. "'Deep in the Heart of Texas,'" I said before I thought.

"I bet a bowl of popcorn it's 'Bewitched, Bothered and Bewildered,'" she said, pouring hot water into the dishpan. "I think we could do the new dance step to that beat. Maybe we could do that for the talent show at Janet's party." The minute I heard that, I knew I was in for a lot of practicing before next Saturday night.

******

It seemed like the dream lasted forever. I'd had it before often enough when I was little, but since I've been in Marshall I've had it several times. It's always the same. There's another baby with me and some woman wearing black is sitting with us. We're swaying and moving around in our seats, and there's a lot of noise coming from below, a constant clickety clack. Children are crying all around me, and I'm scared. Suddenly, the moving stops, and the woman in black takes the other baby and me into a bright room with lots of people talking and poking at us. After a while, I'm back on the seat with the woman in black, and I'm crying. But the other baby isn't there anymore.

When I woke up, my pillow was wet, and I was saying, "No, no," over and over. Then Livy was there shaking me.

"Wake up Shamie. It's only a dream." She put her arms around my shoulders and held me tight until I stopped shaking. "Was it that baby dream again?" Livy asked, turning on the bedside lamp.

I nodded my head and put my feet on the floor. I didn't say anything for a while, and finally I started telling Livy what I'd figured out about the dream. "I think I understand why I've been having that dream since I came to Marshall. I don't know if babies have memories about when they were only two, but I think that part of the dream about shaking and moving was when me and Shannon were on the train coming from New York. And the part that made me cry was when Shannon didn't get back on the train, and I was alone. Maybe the reason I'm having that dream again is because I see Shannon nearly every day at school, and she reminds me of that time."

"You mean, seeing Shannon brings back that memory of you being on the train with her?" I nodded my head but neither one of us said anything for a while. Then she stood up and said, "You go wash your face while I heat some milk," she said, starting down the back stairs. "And take an aspirin while you're in the bathroom."

Naturally I did what Livy told me since she was acting just like Mother. I guess I'm lucky to have a sister that's nearly old enough to be my mother, but most of the time treats me like I'm grownup. When Livy got back with the tray, I noticed she'd brought some graham crackers to dunk in the milk. I don't know if it was the milk that made me feel better or it was being awake and knowing I wasn't alone.

I lay there a long time thinking about that dream, and wondered if I'd have it again now that I understood why I'd been scared. Did Shannon have bad dreams, too? I finally drifted off wondering if she'd ever be glad I was her brother.

Sunday morning we hurried around to fix dinner for the folks since they were coming over right after Sunday School. Livy bought a roast over at Spott's Meat Market, and we'd put potatoes and carrots around it before shoving it in the oven. I'd made a big recipe of Ozark Pudding to impress Mother, and Livy had bought some vanilla ice cream to go with it.

While we ate Sunday dinner, we had a good time getting caught up with all the news, and by the time we finished doing the dishes and cleaning up, it was nearly time for them to go home. It's forty-five miles back to the farm, so Dad always starts home early. Mother gave me $10 to buy myself a new winter jacket and a pair of shoes, and I knew I needed both.

After the folks left I put on my gym shorts under my old gray sweats and walked over to the high school for a run. I was doing the warm-up exercises Pete taught me, when I saw Janet get off her bicycle and start across the lawn toward me. She was wearing one of her brother's baggy red football jerseys over her shorts, but I thought she looked real pretty anyway. She smiled when she saw me and came running over to where I was.

"Hi, Seamus. What are you doing?"

"Warm-up exercises. I'm going to run, and I don't want to get leg cramps or pull a muscle." I answered. "Don't you warm-up before you run?"

"Nobody ever told me I was supposed to, but it looks like a good idea. Will you show me what to do?"

"Sure," I said, and I started showing Janet some of the stretching exercises Pete taught me when I was ten. When we finished, I said, "I'm going to run the cross-country course. It starts here and finishes over at the fairgrounds. You want to run along?"

"Yeah, but I'm surprised you asked. Most boys think I can't keep up. My dumb brother never wants me to run with him."

"Well, let's go. I like to start out slow and build up speed until I can hardly tell I'm running."

Janet nodded like she thought that sounded okay, but she didn't say anything for a while. I could see she was having a good time running on this nice fall day, but she looked like she was getting a little tired. By the time we got to the grandstand, Janet said she thought she'd stop for a rest and told me to go on. So I followed the course around the barns, back to the section where the carnival sets up during the fair, then back toward the grandstand. When I got there, I saw that Janet had company.

Nelson Farris.

He had her backed up against the rail of the grandstand with his arms pinning her in so tight she couldn't move. Janet's face was white, but the look she was giving Farris would of curdled fresh milk. I don't think either one heard me until I gave my karate shout and slapped down hard on Farris's arm.

He didn't say a word, but his face went slack and his arms dropped to his sides. When he saw who'd hit him, he turned red and raised his fist like he was going to kill me. I didn't see a weapon, but if he'd had one, he'd of used it.

"I'd be careful, Farris," I said nice and slow so he'd be sure and understand me. "I have to warn you. I know karate, and I could hurt you. So take off."

He stood there looking meaner than the devil, and then he backed off a step or two and spit at me. Lucky for me, the wind was blowing against him. "I'll kill you for this, you dirty bastard." Then he took off running down the steps and disappeared around the side of the grandstand.

Janet's knees looked like they were going to buckle, so I put my arms out in time to catch her. She hung on to me for a long time while she calmed down.

"Oh, Seamus, I was so scared. He said the nastiest things to me, words I'd never heard before. I didn't think you'd ever get back."

"You're okay now, Janet. Let's sit down a minute." I kept my arm around her because she was still shaking. And besides, I thought she liked it as much as I did. We didn't talk for a while, then, when I thought she was ready to listen, I said, "I hope you won't go out by yourself from now on. He may watch for another chance to get at you. The next time I might not be around."

"Don't worry, I won't. Shannon used to go every place with me, but now Derek's always with her. I don't like to stick myself in where I'm not wanted, but I will now."

"Good," I said, "and I think you ought to tell your folks about this."

"Oh, no. They'd never let me go anyplace if they knew."

"Well, at least tell Derek and Shannon. If you're with them you should be safe." Then I had another idea. "Of course, I could walk with you. If you want me to."

"Oh, Seamus, you're so sweet," she said, and before I knew it, she leaned over and kissed me right on the mouth. I didn't know what to say, but it sure was nice. I reckon she was embarrassed about kissing me because she jumped up and said, "We'd better start home. It's nearly dark."

With the sun gone and a cool breeze blowing, we hurried back to Janet's house. I went all the way up to her door before starting on home. Even though I'm not scared of Farris, I kept my eyes peeled for him because Marshall has a lot of big trees to hide behind. This was the second time he'd threatened me, and I didn't doubt he'd be after me before long. Only I didn't think it would be out in the open. I could almost understand how he felt about being a bastard and all since I'd thought I was one for a long time. I decided I'd better spend more time working on karate than running even though I wanted to get invited to the state invitational this month at Eastern Illinois State Teacher's College. You have to have good low scores to qualify, and so far I had a chance.

I was worried about Janet, too. Farris was crazy about her in his weird way. I hoped she'd tell Derek about him, but I didn't have much hope he'd help. One thing for sure, I wasn't going to worry Livy with this. But by the time I got home, I'd decided to talk to the judge about it.

The Red Headed Girl

Eight: Sneak Attack

Monday after school I was heading for the city library to work on my history report when I heard Scooter yelling at me. "Hey, Seamus, wait for me."

I stopped and waited while Scooter came puffing up the block swinging his book satchel over his shoulder. "Anything wrong?" I asked.

"How come you've never mentioned that you know karate?" he said, catching his breath. He didn't wait for my answer, but went on talking. "On our way home to lunch today Janet told Shannon and me all about what happened yesterday afternoon. She said you arrived just like the cavalry in time to save her."

I nodded my head and started to say something, but Scooter went on. "She really liked the way you warned old Farris about hurting him. That's pretty funny after him scaring the hell out of me all these years."

"I can't stand bullies, and Farris was doing his best to scare Janet. But she didn't let on that he had scared her until after he took off."

"She's got a lot of nerve, all right," Scooter said. We walked along Sixth Street toward Archer with Scooter talking a mile a minute. "I've read that karate has been important in China for hundreds of years and in Japan for a long time, too, but I've never met anyone who knew it. How come you do?"

"I learned it from an old friend named Pete. When he was young, he traveled with a medicine show that wintered in Florida close to the Barnum and Bailey Circus. One day Pete saw a Japanese juggler throw a big roustabout out of his tent. So Pete asked the juggler to teach him."

"So that's it? I didn't think it was something you just picked up on the farm," Scooter laughed. "Think you could teach me?"

"Well, I reckon I could, but it isn't something you can learn in an afternoon. It took me four years to get where I am, and I'm just a beginner. You'd better think it over before you do all that work."

"Maybe I'll just stick close to you," Scooter grinned. "But until now, I've tried not to get guys like Farris pissed off at me," he laughed. "Say, let's go over to Radamaker's, and I'll buy us both one of their famous five-cent ice cream cones."

"Okay, but I can afford to buy my own." When we got inside the store, it was full of kids from school. I didn't know most of their names, but I'd seen 'em around. I was surprised when several called me by name and said hello like I was an old friend. I figured it was because I was with Scooter and everyone knows him. After we found a table and sat down to eat our ice cream, I asked Scooter how he got his nickname.

He grinned and dropped his head like he was embarrassed, but nothing stops him for long. "Well, I had a little red scooter that I rode everywhere when I was young, and when the kids saw me coming, they'd say, `Here comes Billy Schaefer on his scooter.' Then, after a while they just shortened it to, `Here comes Scooter.'" While he was talking, his ice cream started running over the cone, so it took him a while to take care of that, and I had a chance to ask him more about Janet's birthday party.

"It looks like it's going to be smaller than I thought," Scooter said, giving his cone another lick. "Besides the judge and Shannon, it will just be you and your sister, the Radcliffes and me and my folks. Janet didn't think it would be right for us to have a big party with half the world at war."

"That sounds like Janet," I said. "She's a real nice girl."

Scooter grinned like he was in on a big secret and said, "I don't know how you did it, but she's sure sold on you. Why, half the guys in school have crushes on her."

I didn't know how to answer, so I kind of changed the subject and told Scooter I was trying to learn the chorus of "South of the Border" in Spanish. Then he hooted so loud everyone turned around and looked at us.

"Oh, singing a love song isn't enough, you're gonna sing it in Spanish, the language of love." Scooter's usual wide grin got even wider.

I'd finished my ice cream, so I stood up. "If you don't stop acting so dumb, I'm not going to sing at all." I tried to act mad so he'd stop tormenting me. "I'm going to the library and work."

I've been teased all my life about one thing or another. Mostly about my red hair. Lately, it's about being tall and skinny, but I've never been teased about a girl before. I think Janet's real nice to be with, but she makes me feel funny inside, in a way I've never felt before.

Later, when I got home from the library, I had a letter from Mrs. Ashley and a check for $18. She was really excited that I'd found her grandmother's recipe, and she liked the typed copy I sent her. The check would come in handy to buy Christmas presents, but I decided I'd put some of the money with Mother's $10 and get a sheepskin-lined coat. I'd still have enough to buy a pair of Sunday shoes. Maybe I could even get a white shirt to wear under the blue sweater Mother knitted. All the boys wear their shirt collars out over their sweaters, and I wanted to be in style for Janet's party.

After supper while I was doing my schoolwork, the judge called me to talk about Farris' threat to kill me after I rescued Janet. He said Shannon had told him all about it at supper. I was glad Janet had told someone about Farris. Maybe now she'd have someone looking after her if I wasn't around.

"That was good advice you gave Janet about never going anyplace alone," the judge said. "But I think you should follow it, too."

"Oh, I can take care of myself with Farris. He's trying to scare me, but I'm worried about Janet. There's something weird about the way he looks at her when he thinks nobody's watching."

The judge told me Shannon said some nice things about me at supper, but he was careful not to brag on me too much. He wanted Shannon to make up her own mind about me. "She's very fond of Janet, and I think she'd take Farris on herself if he hurt

Janet," the judge said. "I do hope you'll be careful, son. Don't think he'll forget his threat."

"Thanks for calling, but don't worry. I'm not an expert in karate, but I can take care of myself." At that time, I really thought I could.

"Good night, Seamus. I'll see you Saturday night."

After I finished my homework, I wrote to Buster and told him all about life here in Marshall. It was kind of hard to write to him without sounding like I was bragging about what I was doing living in a fancy house and getting paid for the work I was doing. So I laid it on thick about how hard school was and how much I had to study to make good grades.

The next two days, I noticed Shannon didn't rush past when she saw me. Of course, she was always with Derek, and he didn't act any friendlier. In fact, I though he was mad when she talked to me. I wondered if he'd act that way if he knew I was her brother. Janet had kept her word about sticking close to Shannon, and I almost put Farris out of my mind. I was concentrating on cross-country again because we were having a practice run after school. The coach was going to take the top ten runners to Paris on Thursday for the competition between, Casey, Martinsville and Paris, our archrivals.

By now, our Indian summer had almost passed, and the days were getting shorter and shorter. This meant it was nearly dark when we got back to school after practice. I was familiar with the course and even though part of it was in shadows, I wasn't worried about tripping over anything.

At least, not until I got over by the horse barns where the shadows are deepest. That's when my foot caught on something across the path, and down I went. Before I could get up, Nelson Farris landed on me hard with a knife in his hand.

I'd never been threatened with a knife before, so I sucked in my breath in surprise, more likely fear. Well anyway, I went limp like I'd been knocked out. I guess it must of surprised Farris, so he loosened his grip on me just long enough for me to bring my right hand up under his chin and hit him hard, knocking him backwards. Even though I'd had the wind knocked out of me when I fell, I managed to get to my feet before Farris did. I backed off to have room for a kick to his arm, but I didn't like the looks of that knife blade. I'd barely managed to get off a kick to Farris's chest when I was hit from behind. The blow glanced off my shoulder, and I spun around to find Bret Garwood standing there with a thick tree branch in his hands. When my hand chopped down on his arm, he dropped the club and yelled like I'd killed him.

I could hear another runner coming down the path, so I called out to him because he was coming up fast. Even though the light was dim there under the tree, I knew it was Willie Scott, the best runner in school. He barely had time to stop before Farris jumped up in his way.

"What's going on here?" Willie demanded.

"These two tripped me with a rope across the path," I said, catching my breath. While I was talking to Willie, I was watching Farris out of the corner of my eye. He started to grab his knife still there on the ground, and I kicked his arm hard. "Don't even think about it, Farris. The next time I'll aim to hurt." I reached down and picked up the knife. "I'll just take this back to school for you, and you can pick it up in the principal's office."

"You can't do that," he hissed at me. "I'd be kicked out."

"I reckon that's your problem. I don't want any more trouble with you. If you want to fight me, I'll ask the coach to arrange a match in the gym so you can't jump me from behind."

"Come on, Nelson," Bert Garwood said, "Let's get out of here." Garwood didn't wait for an answer but took off across the fairground as fast as he could.

"One of these days, I'll get you Sanford," Farris snarled, "and you'll be sorry you ever messed with me." Then he gave me the nastiest look he could muster and walked off like he'd won the fight.

"What was that all about, Seamus? Why were those two trying to do?" Willie asked.

While I untied the rope from the tree base, I explained everything to Willie. "I figured Bert Garwood was holding the other end of the rope to give Farris a chance to use his knife on me. They'd picked the darkest place on the whole course, a place I couldn't see the rope." Willie just stood there nodding his head while I talked.

"I think I'll just take this rope along with the knife. I'm getting tired of those two dimwits. I'll let the principal take care of 'em."

"Hey, more like the police. Those two were trying to kill you. They shouldn't be running loose," Willie said. "Come on, let's get back to the locker room. I'm cold." We didn't waste any time getting back to school. My shoulder was hurting something awful where I'd been hit by the limb, and my breathing was a little scratchy from falling so hard, but I was anxious to get home. In spite of the delay by the tree, there were still some runners coming along the course behind us.

Mr. Sanders, the cross-country coach, was timing the runners as we came to the school ground, and he looked disappointed that we were off our usual speed. After we explained what had happened, he told us to shower and dress before going to the principal's office.

When we knocked on Mr. Wallace's door a little later, he was cleaning off his desk, nearly ready to go home. He smiled a tired smile and said, "Come in, boys. What's the trouble?" Then he saw the knife and rope in my hands and his face went kind of white. "Where'd you get the knife, Seamus?"

"Nelson Farris tried to use it on me a while ago." Then I explained what happened. "I thought I'd let you take care of this stuff," I said, putting the rope and knife on his desk.

"How did you get into this, Willie?" Mr. Wallace asked.

"I came by after Seamus had everything under control, but those two creeps were still there looking meaner than all get out. I heard everything, and it's just like Seamus said."

Mr. Wallace nodded and said, "I'm afraid this is a matter for the police, boys. It happened after school and off our premises," he said. Then he called the police station and motioned for us to sit down. When he hung up he said, "Chief Vaughn will be over in a few minutes, and he wants you boys to wait. If you'd like to use the phone to call your folks, go right ahead. You can use the phone in my secretary's office."

I called Livy at her school, and she said she'd come by and pick me up after I talked to the chief. It was nearly seven o'clock when we finally got home, and I think Livy was more upset about my narrow escape than I was. She said she was going to the cellar and find a bottle of wine because she needed something "for my stomach's sake and mine other infirmities."

That's in the Bible, but I'd never heard my sister quote it before. Seeing how upset she was I didn't think this was any time to make comments. When Livy started down the cellar steps, I headed out to tend the horses.

When I got back, Livy was heating two cans of store-bought soup and drinking a glass of white wine. "Now, don't you tell Mother, Seamus, but I feel unsettled about this business. What if…." Her voice was kind of choked up and she didn't finish.

"Now, don't worry about what might of happened. The chief is going to come by later and tell us what he found out."

"I'm so thankful you weren't hurt," she said in a shaky voice. "But, I just wish I could have done something to help those boys last year."

"You did as much as anybody could," I said and patted Livy's arm. "Too bad they didn't have a father like ours." Livy nodded and got up to stir the soup. We didn't say much while we ate. In spite of all the excitement, I managed to eat two bowls of soup and a few slices of bread and butter. After we cleaned up the dishes, I got out my guitar. Strumming on it seems to ease my mind, but tonight it was keeping my fingers from trembling.

It was nearly nine o'clock when Chief Vaughn knocked on the kitchen door. He'd come around back since the front of the house was dark.

"Well, son," he said, taking off his hat when he stepped into the kitchen, "it looks like both boys have disappeared. Farris's grandparents saw him leaving the house before his mother got home from the shoe factory, but they didn't talk to him. I expect he's hit the road, maybe looking for that band of gypsies that camp on their farm every summer."

"What about Bert Garwood?" I asked the chief.

"Gone, just like Farris. He may be with Farris, or more likely gone to his mother in Indianapolis. At least that's what his grandpa thinks." The chief looked around the kitchen before he went on. "Now, you understand, all this is just what we think. They could both be hid out around here someplace. So, if I was you, I'd be mighty careful."

"I'd figured on that, but I'd just as soon you didn't mention this to my sister. She's really upset, so I'll let her think they've lit out for good."

The chief nodded and put on his hat. "But if you hear anything about either one, call me right away. I'll have my patrolman swing by here a few times a night and flash his lights around." He pointed to Duke curled up in his bed next to Stormy and laughed. "Better leave that fierce watchdog out at night. Might bark if he heard something."

Thursday morning during the announcements, Mr. Wallace told the students that Nelson Farris and Bert Garwood were wanted for questioning by the police and asked everyone to be on the look out for 'em. He didn't go into any details about what they'd tried to do, but he didn't need to. Everyone had heard what happened. In fact, I think the story had grown considerable during the night. I didn't much like the attention, but everyone in the whole school knew who I was by the end of the day.

The cross-country team left for Paris before school was out, the town being thirteen miles from Marshall. We were all steamed up since Martinsville and Casey were going to be there, too. Usually our school's not much interested in the cross-country team, but some of the girls that know us decided it would cheer us on to victory if they came and watched. Janet and Shannon rode over with Willie Scott's sister. She's one of the cheerleaders, so the other two cheerleaders came along all dressed up in their uniforms.

The day was a whole lot brighter and warmer than Wednesday, so everyone was in a good mood. Teachers from all four schools were stationed around the course recording times, so I could keep my mind on the race and not worry about booby traps along the way.

Since my scores were pretty low this season, I had a good starting position. I don't like to push myself much at first, so a few runners passed me right away. I just moved along steady-like and paced myself with the speed of the Marshall boys. I knew who I'd have to pass to make a good show, and I gradually picked up speed. We'd passed the two and a half mile mark when I got close to Willie. That was when I speeded up and started passing most of the other runners. Just as I came in sight of the finish line, I took a big breath and spent the last bit of energy I'd been saving.

I could hardly believe it when I heard the coach say, "Third," as I passed by. When I slowed down just past the finish line, I saw Janet and Shannon waving their arms and yelling my name. I don't think I'd ever felt so proud.

The Red Headed Girl

Nine: The Party

Friday after school Livy took me to Terre Haute to the Sears & Roebuck store and helped me pick out some new clothes. I got a brown wool, sheepskin-lined coat with a lambskin collar for $8.95. The one I really wanted was leather and cost twice as much, but I knew I was lucky to have a warm coat that had inside knit cuffs to keep the wind from blowing up the sleeves.

I guess the leather coat was just a dream like the pair of high-top boots I wanted when I was ten. I also picked out a new white shirt and pair of brown leather loafers that cost $2.98. I'd never bought so many new clothes before, but I only had to add four dollars of my own money to the ten Mother gave me.

After we picked out my clothes, we went to the ladies department to look for Janet's birthday present. I wanted to buy her an identification bracelet like everyone's wearing these days, but they cost more than I could afford. I finally decided on a bottle of Evening in Paris perfume with an atomizer on the top. It came in a gift box and looked real expensive. When Livy said she liked that kind of perfume, that was good enough for me. As I was handing the clerk my $1.75, I couldn't help thinking how long it took me to earn that much money at twenty-five cents an hour. It was a lot of money, but Janet was worth every penny.

Saturday morning I woke up thinking about going to Janet's birthday party, hoping I wouldn't do anything to embarrass myself. I was glad I had a lot of work to keep my mind off it. I raked up the last of the fall leaves, and burned them while I cleaned the stables and put down fresh bedding for the horses. Since the feed store had sent out a new load of alfalfa and grain, I had to stack it in the end of the stable.

Now that winter's nearly here I have to keep the stoker of the fancy Hercules hot air furnace filled. It holds 350 pounds, so I only have to do it once a day. It isn't near as much work as the heating stove on the farm because the coal is automatically fed into the furnace firebox. Besides, the coal is right there in the basement, and I don't have to go to the shed and get it a bucket at a time.

Even so, I still have plenty to do to keep it working. I reckon all this talk about furnaces is pretty dull for most folks, but it's mighty interesting to a person that grew up carrying in coal faster than he carried out the ashes.

We've shut off most of the heat to the bedrooms upstairs to save fuel. With the war news getting worse and worse, President Roosevelt's asking us to make sacrifices and save our resources for the military. It's no problem for us because we spend most of our time in the kitchen anyway.

That evening when we got to the Radcliffe's house, Scooter and his folks were already there. I could see through the window that he was messing with the floor-model radio and phonograph, so I figured he'd brought some of his records to play at the party.

I sure was glad Scooter was there because I hardly ever need to say anything with him around. I was feeling awful self-conscious, wondering if I could think of anything to say to Janet's folks when I got inside.

When Mr. Radcliffe opened the door, he said hello to Livy before he shook my hand. Then he put his arm over my shoulder like he was glad to see me. I'd never met him before, and I was surprised to see how friendly he was.

"Glad to meet you, son. Janet's told us all about how you put that Nelson Farris to flight." I wondered if she'd told her folks about Farris scaring her last Sunday or just about trying to knife me on

Wednesday. "Here, Seamus, let me take your coat," Mr. Radcliffe said, closing the door.

Janet came down the stairs just then, and she was all dressed up in a gold colored velvet dress with a little ruffled collar. Livy told me later it was a princess style because it was fitted real smooth until it flared out at the hem. I'd never seen Janet in anything but loose sweaters, and I couldn't help noticing what a nice shape she had. It was the kind of figure that makes boys want to whistle. I guess I must have looked dumbstruck standing there staring at her. I almost forgot I had her present in my hand, but she didn't seem to notice. She just smiled at me and said, "Hello, Seamus, I'm glad you could come."

"Happy Birthday," I said, giving her the present. "I hope you like it." I knew we were talking in a funny sort of way like folks do at weddings or funerals, all formal-like but not really saying anything. I figured we'd get back to every-day talk after we got used to seeing each other all dressed up.

"I love it," Janet said as she held the box near her nose and sniffed. Then she put it on the library table with the other presents. Her cheeks were flushed and pink and she was smiling at me in a different kind of way.

Suddenly I noticed Scooter had started the record player and was standing next to me trying to introduce his parents. It wasn't long until Derek and Shannon came in the front door followed by the judge, so the party started getting lively.

"So where's your guitar, Seamus?" Scooter asked me. He'd put a Gene Autry song on the record player, and I figured he'd done it to make me feel at home.

"I left it in the car," I said, "but I'll go get it when you're ready for me to sing. What are you going to do for the entertainment?"

"Just you wait and see," he said. He grinned and his eyes lit up like he knew a joke he couldn't wait to tell."

It wasn't long until Janet's mother came in to call us to supper. She'd arranged the food on the buffet, and we were to help ourselves and sit wherever we wanted. She told Janet to go first, being the guest of honor and all. Janet took my hand and pulled me along behind her, and called to Scooter over her shoulder, "Come on, let's eat." Janet smiled at me like she understood how out-of-place I felt at the head of the line.

We filled our plates and Janet led us into the living room. "Here, let's sit on the couch and we'll put our food on the coffee table." It wasn't long until Derek and Shannon came in, too. Everyone must have been hungry because we didn't say much while we plowed through baked beans, potato salad and sliced ham. Even Scooter was quiet for a while.

After he finished, he started telling me about the Silvertone phonograph-radio combination he was going to use during the entertainment. He showed me the black microphone with the flat base that he wanted me to sing into. He said the speakers on the phonograph would amplify the music and make it sound like it was coming from the radio.

"But I've never used a microphone before," I told him. I didn't like the idea of trying new equipment and a new song at the same time. "I think everyone can hear me just fine without a microphone."

"Now, Seamus, you just follow directions," Scooter said, putting his hand on my shoulder, "and I'll only make you sing one song." Then he got up to put another stack of records on before he went back to the dining room for seconds.

Before long, Mrs. Radcliffe called us all into the dining room for the cake cutting. The big white cake was decorated with yellow roses and had fourteen yellow candles on it. After lighting the candles,

Janet's mother turned off the overhead light and everyone sang happy birthday. Janet's face was pink with excitement, and I thought she was about the prettiest girl I'd ever seen. We all clapped when Janet blew out the candles, then her mother turned on the lights and cut the cake.

After dessert, Janet opened her presents, and I could tell she liked everything a lot. Her folks gave her a gold heart locket, Shannon gave her an ankle bracelet, and Derek gave her a Brownie box camera. When she opened my present she looked at me and smiled. "Oh, my favorite."

After she'd opened all the presents, Scooter said it was time for the program, and he told Janet she'd get his present a little later. While I went to the car to get my guitar, Derek opened the sliding oak doors into the library and carried in some extra chairs, so the adults took their coffee in there.

With Janet's presents cleared off the library table, Scooter put the microphone on it and pulled a chair next to it so I could sit down. I took my guitar out of the case and checked the strings before I sat down to play. Scooter made sure the mike was working when he introduced my song, then went back to the phonograph, flipped a switch and nodded to me to start.

I strummed a few cords like Gene Autry does before he starts singing and everyone quieted down. I glanced at Janet when I thought she wasn't looking, and she had a tiny smile on the corners of her lips but a big smile sparkled in her eyes. When I started singing the first verse I just put everyone but Janet out of my mind and sang the words for her. By the time I got to the chorus that I'd been practicing in Spanish all week, I felt the words roll off my tongue as if I understood 'em.

When I finished, everyone clapped like they liked it. "That was wonderful, Seamus," Janet said. "You sound like the singer in the movie at the Pythian Theatre last week."

"Yeah, and he's better looking," Scooter added, taking a record off the phonograph. "And here's your present, Janet. Hot from the recording studio. Want to hear it?"

I didn't know what to think when Scooter put on the record, and there was my voice singing "South of the Border" right over the speakers. I guess I must have looked dumbfounded because I heard Derek laugh and slap his knee like he'd seen something awful funny. I didn't like the smartass look on his face because I knew he was laughing at me.

When the record was over, Derek looked at me and asked, "What's the matter, Seamus. Haven't you ever heard of home recording?"

"I don't reckon I have. We don't have electricity on the farm, so we don't have a record player." Right then, I felt like the dumbest boob that ever lived.

Then I heard Livy's voice coming from the other room. "Janet, the Ashleys have a home recorder on their phonograph, and if you'd like Seamus to record a song on the other side, I'm sure he can figure it out."

You could have heard a pin drop until Scooter put a new record on, and said, "This is your song, Derek. I believe you're going to do your Bing Crosby imitation." He handed Derek the microphone and looked at Shannon. He pointed at his watch to tell her that her dance was next on the program. When Shannon started up the stairs to put on her costume, Derek took the microphone and stood up. I wasn't sure why he needed it because he just moved his mouth and tried to look like he was singing the words to "I Don't Want to Set the World on Fire." Even though he was just pretending to sing, it wasn't hard to tell when he forgot the words. I couldn't help feeling a little happy when he got mixed up so bad he had to stop mouthing the words until Bing got to the chorus. When the record was over, we all clapped, but I could tell I wasn't the only one that didn't have his heart in it.

Scooter told us that Shannon was going to do her dance next, and the ones in the living room would have to move into the library to make room for the dance. After I helped Scooter roll up the living room rug and move back the furniture, I sat down on the floor in front of the judge.

When Scooter could see Shannon on the landing of the circular stairs, he explained that this dance was from the Cinderella ballet. The story would start just after her two stepsisters left for the ball and made Cinderella stay at home and work.

Scooter had fixed up an old desk lamp with a flexible arm to make a spotlight. After he started the music, he pointed the light on the stairs where Shannon was waiting. With the living room lights off, it worked real fine.

The record started with a loud bang on the drums, like a door being slammed. The music was sad as Shannon danced into the room wearing a tattered apron over an old brown dress, her hair tied back in a kerchief. The spotlight followed Shannon as she danced around the room and stopped in front of the fireplace. For a second the light went out, then the spotlight moved across the mantle and came to rest on a picture. I was sure it was Shannon's mother from the way she looked at it. While Shannon stood there in front of the fireplace with tears running down her face, the music gradually got louder. Finally, she put the picture back on the mantle, picked up the broom and started to sweep.

Then music got livelier and Shannon stopped in the middle of the floor to wipe her eyes on her apron. As she straightened her shoulders, a smile flickered across her face like she was thinking of something nice. By now, the orchestra was playing a waltz, and I imagined Cinderella was thinking of the prince's ball. Suddenly Shannon pulled off her scarf, and her red hair fell around her face like a halo. Even in her ragged clothes she looked like a princess.

With the music getting happier and happier, she flipped the broom over on the end and tied her scarf around the brush. Then she nodded her head like the broom was a dance partner and waltzed around the room. When the music stopped Shannon bowed and smiled, then Scooter turned off his spotlight. For a while, nobody made a sound, and then we started clapping for all we were worth.

I knew it had only been dark a few minutes, but it was long enough to see my sister in a different light. I suddenly understood what a terrible time she'd had since her mother died. Even though I'd never lost anyone, I could put myself in Shannon's place. Just thinking about losing Mother or Dad or Livy was too much for me.

I didn't know I was crying until the judge put his hand on my shoulder and gave me his handkerchief. When I watched Shannon's face as she danced, I saw our mother's face. I thought how sad she must have been to know she wouldn't live to see us grow up. Even though I felt sad, I was happy, too. Shannon's dance was beautiful, and I knew she had a tender heart I'd never seen before.

I guess Scooter understood the mood we were in, so he put on Livy's new record and said it was time to go south of the border. Livy jumped up from her chair like she couldn't wait to start dancing. She gave me a hand up, and we started doing the new step just like we'd practiced it in the kitchen. The dance seemed a lot fancier now with Livy's long, full skirt swirling around as we twisted and turned to the Latin beat. It's pretty hard to be sad while you're dancing to that music, so I had as much fun as Livy. I've always been proud to be Livy's brother, but never as proud as I was tonight.

It was midnight by the time we thanked the Radcliffes for the party. Livy hugged Janet and told her we expected her after lunch the next afternoon so I could record another song on her record. Her father said he'd drop her off at two o'clock when he went down to his office to do some work.

The next day when Janet rang the front door bell, she was wearing a yellow twin sweater set with her gold heart locket around her neck. She handed me the record Scooter made for her and held up her new camera and said, "Before we go inside, I want to take your picture, Seamus." So we went out into the sunshine and took pictures until Janet was satisfied there was at least one good one. Then we went inside.

That morning I'd read the instructions on the Ashley's phonograph about how to make records and felt I could do it without any trouble. We talked for a while about what song she wanted me to sing and finally decided on "The Yellow Rose of Texas." I told Janet she made me think of that song every time she wore yellow, so I wondered if that was what made her decide.

After I recorded the song and played it back to see if it sounded okay, we went in the kitchen to make hot chocolate. We talked about her party for a while, and Janet kind of apologized for the way her brother acted for laughing at me about not knowing about the home recorder. Then she got quiet and thoughtful for a while. Finally she told me why.

"Derek is really mad at you. He thinks Shannon likes you more than she does him."

"That's pretty funny since she practically doesn't know I'm alive. What makes him think that?"

"I guess it was because she asked you to show her how to do that new dance step. He was watching every move you made."

"Shannon sure is a good dancer. She caught on real fast."

"Yes, she's always been good at dancing," Janet said, kind of sad-like. "I could tell you liked to dance with her, and you looked so nice together. You looked like that pair of porcelain figurines that Shannon's father gave her for her birthday." Janet got up and put her cup in the sink, and while she had her back turned to me, she asked in a shaky voice. "Do you like dancing with Shannon better than you do me?"

At first, I couldn't think why Janet had asked that. "Of course not," I told her, and I went over to the sink and put my arm around her waist. I could tell she was upset, standing there all stiff-like. I just stood next to her without saying anything. Not knowing much about girls, it took me a while to understand what was wrong. Finally, I figured it out.

Janet didn't know Shannon was my sister, but she'd noticed I'd always looked sad when Shannon treated me like I was a country hick. She thought I liked Shannon like a girlfriend. "You have the wrong idea, Janet. If I told you something, something very private, would you promise not to tell Shannon?"

"Of course, but I don't understand."

"Well, I don't know if Livy told you, but I'm adopted like Shannon is, and we both came to Illinois on the Orphan Train when we were two years old." Janet looked kind of confused about what I'd just said. "Well, to tell you the truth, I didn't know I had a twin sister until the Rawleigh man told me there was a red-headed girl living in Marshall that was the spittin' image of me."

"Seamus, you don't mean Shannon's your twin sister?"

"That's right, but she doesn't know, and I don't want her to. Not yet."

"This is so hard to believe. And you've been living so close all this time. Does the judge know?"

"Yeah, Livy told him all about it before I came here, and he's been awful good to me."

"Well, this explains a lot of things to me. I don't know how you can be so sweet and patient with Shannon when she hasn't been nice to you at all." Janet paused and looked at me before she went on. "You know, I didn't understand why I liked you so much, right from the start. Now that I know you're related, I can see you look alike. And you both move so gracefully, like cats. Janet stopped talking for a second, and then went on.

"Even though she's been real different since her mother died, I love Shannon like a sister. We've always been best friends." She looked up at me and her smile kind of quivered as she said, "Oh, Seamus, this is all so unbelievable, but I'm glad you told me. I really thought Derek was right, that you liked Shannon and you just liked me because I was always with her."

Sometimes it's hard for me to understand girls even though I have more sisters than a boy needs. But Janet's different. She just says what she thinks and doesn't hem 'n haw around about it.

"Seamus, if I get a good picture of you on my new camera, would you mind if I put it in my locket?"

Ten: Thanksgiving

October drifted into November, and almost before I noticed, winter had set in. The days were short and dark. It seemed like the war news from Europe was as dark and depressing as the days. Everywhere we looked there were posters about donating blood to the Red Cross and buying war bonds. There was one with the slogan, "Loose Lips Sink Ships."

But I knew it wasn't loose lips that sank our destroyer the Reuben James three weeks earlier. It was a torpedo from a German submarine. The Reuben James was escorting unarmed merchant ships bound for England, and President Roosevelt got on the radio to address the American people. He called it an "unprovoked attack."

Everyone agreed it was just a matter of time before we got into the war hot and heavy. And for sure the sinking of that first American ship brought the war home to folks in Marshall because a hometown boy died on it. It was weird that such an awful thing happened on Halloween night when the local boys had nothing more important in mind than turning over outhouses and finding other mischief to get into.

After our ship sunk, it seemed like war was all folks could think of. There were scrap metal drives, war bond rallies. The Red Cross held meetings to fold bandages and teach first aid and home nursing.

But while the adults all worried about the war they knew was coming, us kids went on with our schoolwork and other things kids do. I guess that was because we didn't know anything else to do. It hadn't happened to us yet, and after all, it was still on the other side of the ocean. I tried not to think about it because I was going home to the farm to spend a few days.

School let out early Wednesday afternoon for Thanksgiving vacation, and I took the Greyhound bus to Greenup. Dad picked me up at Peg's Diner where the bus stops, and we headed home. Livy didn't come because the Ashleys were home from Washington, D.C for a few days on business, and she stayed in Marshall to visit with them.

When we got to Toledo, Dad drove around the courthouse square so I could see if there had been any changes since I'd been gone. But everything looked about the same. Woolen's Drugstore had put a new Coke sign in the window, and I could see a few customers in the Rainbow Cafe. It was too early for the theater to open, and the First National Bank was closed for the day. When we drove by the Toledo Democrat, Jim Drakeford was locking up, and he waved to us. Connell's grocery store had a few customers, but it looked like most folks had gone home for supper.

Dad turned off the square on Meridian Street, and we headed toward the gravel road that folks around here call the Burma Road because they say it's as bad as the one that goes from Burma to China. In rainy weather it's just two sets of ruts going north and two sets going south, but now it was dusty and it felt like we were driving over a washboard.

"I guess things haven't changed much since I've been gone," I said, looking at the farms as we drove by. "But it sure feels like it's been a long time."

"It seems that way to Mother and me, too. The old place ain't the same without you. She could hardly sleep last night for thinking about you coming home."

I got a lump in my throat just thinking about Mother. I knew she'd been lonely without me. All these years, there'd always been a young one at home, now we were all gone. I thought she deserved more time to rest, but I guess there was emptiness in the house with Alvina and me both gone. Not that I'm especially fond of Alvina, but I couldn't help wondering how she was getting along in the WAVES.

"What do you hear from Alvina?" I asked Dad. Alvina's a mighty selfish girl, but she loves Dad more than anyone. And he's real partial to her.

"The little rascal joined the WAVES without so much as a by-your-leave, but she's happier than a lark." He laughed before he added slowly, "or so she says. She called last night to tell us to meet her at the train station in Mattoon tomorrow."

"I suppose she's changed some since I saw her last year when she left for Chicago?"

"Well, I don't know about that since she's not much for writing, but I reckon she's doing things the navy way now whether she likes it or not," Dad chuckled and jerked the steering wheel to miss a big chuck hole in the road.

"Does she still hear from John Mason?"

"She didn't say, but I reckon he'll be home from the university for Thanksgiving," Dad said, turning east on the Bradbury road and the last four miles home. As we came to the hill near Cottonwood Creek, I wondered if I'd see Mary Ruth Mason when we passed their big white house at the top. Dad must have known what I was thinking because he looked at me and grinned, then gave the horn three short beeps as we passed the house. "Looking for Mary Ruth, are you?" He laughed in his teasing way and said, "She always asks us about you when we see her."

As we passed Jones School I could see little wisps of smoke coming from the chimney like the teacher had banked the fire, but there wasn't a soul around. I couldn't help thinking about Buster trying to get my dinner bucket that first day of school four years ago. Now he's a mechanic on the U.S.S West Virginia in Pearl Harbor. It was hard to believe I hadn't seen him for two years.

We pulled up in front of the house, and Bobbie came out to meet us, barking like she knew I was in the cab. When I opened the truck door, she let out a happy yelp. I picked her up to rub her ears, and she licked me on the face a few times before I put her down. Then I grabbed my suitcase and Mother's package and hurried to the back porch where she was waiting at the kitchen door. I leaned down to kiss her, and she gave me a bear hug like she hadn't seen me for a year.

"My oh, my, Seamus. It seems like you've been gone so long," Mother said with a happy sigh. "I bet you've grown an inch since September."

I tightened my arms around her and lifted her off her feet. "But I haven't grown since you saw me last," I said, putting her back down.

I could hear Dad coming up the steps with Bobbie barking at his heels, and he called to Mother to get the milk buckets ready while he changed his clothes.

"That man," Mother said, "he worries more about his cows than he does me. The buckets have been washed and ready since the milking this morning. She walked over to the cook-stove and shoved another stick of wood in before lifting the lid off a big pot on the back of the stove. When she turned around to look at me, she smiled and said, "We're having chicken and noodles for supper."

I handed Mother my package and said, "I brought you something."

She opened the box and smiled as she took out two tortoise shell combs decorated with rhinestones across the top. "Why, Seamus, they're just about the prettiest combs I've ever seen." Then she went to the mirror over the washstand and put one on each side of her hair. "There, that should take care of the hair that's always sliding into my eyes." She turned to look at the side and replaced a white hairpin that had slipped from the thick bun at the back of her head. It was the most time I'd ever seen her spend in front of a mirror.

"I'm glad you like 'em. When I saw them in the window of Casteel's Dry Goods store, I thought they looked just like you." I could hear Dad gathering up the buckets on the screened porch and asking Mother, "You reckon Maudie will let me milk her tonight?"

"It's been a while," Mother laughed, "but I guess you still have gentle hands."

That night after supper Pete came over and brought his fiddle, so we played a few tunes together with Dad on the piano and me on my guitar. After we finished, I told them about making a phonograph record, and Mother could hardly believe it. Right then, I decided I'd get her a wind-up record player for Christmas and make a record for her. I saw a phonograph in the catalog for $7.35, so I'd skimp on some of the other presents if I had to.

In a little while, Mother said good night and went to bed because she had to get up early to start cooking for Thanksgiving. But she told Pete not to hurry off so we could visit. It wasn't long until Dad went to bed, too. That's when I started telling Pete all about keeping up with my karate practice. Mostly, I wanted to tell him about Nelson Farris trying to knife me, but I sure didn't want my folks to know about it. I also wanted to thank him again for teaching me karate so I could look after myself.

"Yes, sir," Pete said, nodding his head as he listened to me, "I don't know what I'd have done if I hadn't been able to defend myself when I was traveling with the medicine show. I met up with a lot of tough guys in the places we went." Pete leaned over and put his fiddle in the case and snapped the latch before he went on talking. "I've been teaching karate to your friend Billie Joe Neff. I can see that it's given him a lot of self-confidence." Pete paused a second before saying, "The Neff's are living on my place and farming for me now, so I see Billy Joe most every day"

"That's great. I don't know what they'd have done if you hadn't helped his mother when they were so hard up four years ago. All they had to live on was what his dad made working on the WPA."

"Times were bad for a lot of folks then," Pete said.

I've always admired Pete, but I didn't realize until tonight how much it meant to have a grown-up man for a friend. One who'd listen to what I had to say without finding fault, and didn't give advice until I asked for it. Even when I was little he'd listen to me patient-like, as though what I had to say was the most important thing in the world. Having Pete for a friend is real special to me.

The next morning after we finished the chores, Mother asked me if I wanted to go to the station with Dad to pick up Alvina. "There isn't room for four of us in the cab of the truck," she said, "and I have a lot of cooking to do. And besides, your Aunt Jenny's coming early to help me."

So we set out for town to pick up Alvina at the Mattoon train station. The Illinois Central starts up around Chicago and goes clear to New Orleans. The New York Central comes from the east, but I don't know how far west it goes. I do know the two railroads cross in Mattoon, and their stations are just a block apart. So there's a lot of activity around Mattoon these days with trains carrying troops and war supplies in all directions.

The day was cold and windy, but we decided to wait out on the platform for the City of New Orleans to come in. Dad was anxious to see Alvina, and I guess he thought the train would get there faster if he was out on the platform. I was glad I was wearing my new coat and hoped I looked good enough to keep Alvina from making smart remarks about my clothes. She always found something to criticize me about.

Every few minutes Dad looked at his watch, then he'd put it back in his pocket and stared down the tracks to see if the train was coming. Finally, we heard it whistle as it came under the Dewitt street bridge a few blocks north of the station, and then the brakes squeaking as it slowed to a stop.

After the conductor climbed down and put the stepbox on the ground, he held out his arm to help a woman down the steps. It took a while for me to recognized Alvina in the navy uniform. Her dark hair was in a bun tucked under her cap. She looked grown-up and kind of glamorous, and the full-length overcoat made her seem taller and thinner. After she got off, three sailors came down behind her carrying suitcases. At first I thought she'd invited them home for the holiday because they were making such a big fuss over her. While all this was going on, Alvina didn't look around. She just kept talking to the sailors. When the train started moving the men jumped back on, she stood there waving at them.

Finally, she turned around and saw us. Dad started grinning and walking toward her, and she ran to him, her arms stretched out like she was glad to see him. When she saw me, she kind of blinked like she didn't recognize me. "My God, is that you Seamus?"

"I reckon so," I said, not knowing what else to say to such a dumb question.

Alvina studied me a second before she said any more. "You must have grown a foot since I last saw you. Why, you're practically a man." She hugged Dad again and started over to get her suitcases. Then she remembered me. "Go get my luggage, Seamus. Make yourself useful," she said. I knew then the only thing different about Alvina was her uniform.

It was nearly eleven o'clock when we got home, and two cars were parked in front of the house. One belonged to Aunt Minnie and Uncle Joe, some folks that go to our church but don't have any family around here. I call them aunt and uncle on account of their being old, not because we're related. Mother invites them to our house on holidays.

The other car was Aunt Jenny's, Mother's youngest sister. After she got divorced and moved to Toledo, she opened a beauty shop in her front room.

I put Alvina's suitcases in her room and headed toward the kitchen to see what was going on. But Aunt Minnie and Uncle Joe were sitting by the heating stove in the dining room, so I sat down to visit with them. Alvina was already in the kitchen talking to Aunt Jenny and Mother. I could hear Alvina making a fuss over how good everything looked. Since she was being so nice, I knew she wanted Mother to do something for her. It wasn't long until I heard Alvina say she'd brought her uniforms home, and they all needed to be taken in a bit.

A little later when Mother had everything on the table she called us to eat. After smelling all that food cooking, I was hungrier than usual. I don't think there's a better cook in all of Cumberland County than Mother.

A lot of folks have turkey for Thanksgiving, but we were having a capon that Mother'd raised from a chick. Capons are roosters that have been neutered so they'll grow to twice their normal size. When I was little and Chicken Tommy came to caponize, I used to ask him what he was doing to the roosters. He'd just grin and say he was taking their tonsils out so they'd grow big and strong.

After Dad asked a blessing on the food, we started passing the dishes around the big oak table, and for a while it looked like a merry-go-round with all the dishes going by. Besides the capon, there were mashed potatoes and gravy, candied sweet potatoes, green beans, dressing and cranberry sauce. And best of all, hot rolls and butter. I was glad when everything had been passed so we could settle down to eating.

"I'd almost forgot how good your cooking is, Mother," I said after I'd tasted everything. It's even better than I remembered."

"Thank you, Seamus. It's mighty good to have you home," Mother smiled. "And I'm glad to have you, too, Alvina."

"How's food in the mess hall, Alvina?" Dad asked.

"It isn't anything like this, but it's not bad," Alvina grinned.

We hadn't even got to the pumpkin pie and whipped cream when the phone rang a long and three shorts, our ring. Alvina jumped up to answer before anyone else had a chance. And sure enough, it was for her.

"How did you know I was here?" she asked into the phone. I couldn't hear the answer, but Alvina nodded her head and said, "Sure, I'll be ready."

After she hung up, she turned around and said, "That was John Mason. He and Patty want me to come over and tell them all about the WAVES. They'll be here in a few minutes, so I hope you'll excuse me while I go freshen up." I could tell the way she said it she was doing her best to be polite.

We all just sat there looking at her without saying anything. Mother and Dad looked real disappointed that she was leaving so soon, but I wasn't surprised. She always managed to get out of work somehow, and Mother's kitchen looked like it needed at least an hour of dish washing to put it to rights.

With Aunt Jenny helping me, we finally cleared the kitchen and put everything away. Then, she took a few leftovers and headed back to town. It wasn't long until Aunt Minnie and Uncle Joe went home, and Mother and Dad both fell asleep in their chairs.

It was so quiet I decided to go for a bicycle ride, so I left a note on the kitchen table to let Mother know where I was going. I got out my beat-up old bike from the coal shed and started peddling down the road. While I rode down that familiar gravel road towards Jones School, I wondered what Buster was doing today. That was when I decided to ride over to his house and say hello to his mother.

When I knocked on the door a little later, Mrs. Johnson looked at me like she didn't know who I was. She stood there staring at me a few seconds before she asked, "You can't be the Sanford boy," her voice trailed off in a question. I smiled at her and stuck out my hand. "My goodness, it is you, Seamus. But you're all grown up. Come in and tell me what you've been doing."

The first thing I saw when I walked into the room was Buster's picture on the table next to Mrs. Johnson's rocking chair. He was wearing his uniform and smiling into the camera. I hardly recognized him because his skin had cleared up, and he'd lost weight. I had to admit with that smile on his face, he was a good-looking guy. "My goodness, Buster sure has changed," I said, and I was glad Mrs. Johnson couldn't read my mind.

She nodded and sat down in the rocking chair. "I miss him a whole lot, but I'm glad he got out of this place." She stopped to look at me like she'd remembered Buster's school days. "I'm real sorry he was nasty to you, but he didn't know no better with his brothers shoving him around and telling him how dumb he was. It's a wonder he turned out as good as he did."

"He wrote me a letter and told me he was sorry," I said, wanting to put her mind at ease. "He said he was lonesome and didn't hear from anyone but you. I thought I'd stop and see you so I could tell him about it in my next letter."

Before Mrs. Johnson could say anything, Jimmy Ray stumbled into the room. It didn't take a minute to see that he'd been celebrating Thanksgiving with a whiskey bottle, and it hadn't improved his manners a bit. "What you doin' sniffin' around here, you little red-headed bastard?"

I didn't know if Jimmy Ray remembered who I was, but it was plain he didn't want me around. He lurched over and caught hold of the end of the couch, so I stood up to be ready for whatever he had in mind. "If you're going to talk like that, just get back outside," Mrs. Johnson said. I could tell she was embarrassed and mad at the same time.

He drew back his arm and started toward his mother like he was going to hit her. I didn't wait to see what he'd decided but I stepped out and flipped him over using his outstretched arm like a pump handle. Jimmy Ray landed in the middle of the room with a thud. A look of amazement spread over his face, but it turned to pure hate as he struggled to his feet.

"If I was you, Jimmy Ray, I'd go sleep it off. I don't want to hurt you, but I won't let you hit your mother." I was poised and ready in case he decided to get really nasty, and I must have looked more convincing that I felt. For a minute he couldn't decide what to do, but he finally headed back outside. I don't like shoving anyone around, especially in front of his mother, so I was glad he didn't ask for any more trouble. I eased back into the chair, but I was ready to head home where people didn't get drunk and fight.

"I'm real sorry about that, Seamus. He's been drafted and has to report for his physical next week. I know that's no excuse for him, but he's scared. I just hope the army can do something with him," she said with a heavy sigh. "God knows, I never could."

I didn't know what to say to Mrs. Johnson, but I felt mighty sorry for her. Living here with her miserable husband and son had made her a pitiful sight. "Why do you stay here?" I asked her suddenly. "Why don't you leave 'em and get a job in a defense plant? They need workers real bad right now."

Tears started running down her face, and she wiped them away with the back of her hand. "That's what Buster said when he left. He was tired of fighting back and getting nowhere. That's why he joined up. As long as he seemed destined to fight, he said he'd be better off doing it for his country."

Saturday night after John Mason took Alvina to Mattoon to catch the train back to Chicago, it seemed like old times at home. Mother and Dad studied their Sunday school lessons by the heating stove while I worked on my Spanish. My teacher, Mr. Vadas, asked me to bring my guitar to class so I could sing "South of the Border" since I'd learned the chorus in Spanish. He liked it so much he gave me the words to some Christmas carols in Spanish. He says memorizing words to songs is a real good way to learn a language.

Even though I was studying, I couldn't help but watch Dad trying to stay awake so he could read his lesson. He'd slap himself every now and then and read a little more before his eyes closed. Finally, he laid his head back on the chair and fell asleep. Mother looked at him and smiled, then put her Bible on the table.

"What do you say we go make some hot chocolate before we fall asleep, too?" We got up quiet-like so we wouldn't wake Dad. Mother walked outside to the screened porch, our icebox this time of the year, and got the milk. When she came back she said, "It seems like I've been so busy fitting Alvina's uniforms we haven't had a minute to talk."

I got out the sugar and Hershey's cocoa from the pantry and measured them out in a cup for Mother. "I'd of thought there would be folks on the base to take in her uniforms," I said. "She shouldn't have brought all of them home for you to do." I couldn't help feeling resentful.

"Well, you know Alvina," Mother said with a nod of her head. Since Mother never wastes anything, not even words, she didn't say anymore about Alvina. "I've been wondering about your twin sister. You haven't said much about her."

I stood there thinking how to tell mother about Shannon when I didn't really understand her myself. "She's hard to figure," I said, shaking my head. "So far, she hasn't paid much attention to me. Naturally, she doesn't know I'm her brother, but I hope some day things will be different. Well, you know..." I couldn't put into words what I wanted to say, but I figured Mother'd understand anyway.

"I reckon it's real hard for you," Mother said, putting her hand on my shoulder, "wanting to tell her all you know about being in the orphanage, 'n all the things we learned from the Sisters in New York." Mother stirred a little milk into the cocoa and sugar before she poured it into the hot milk.

"Yeah, it's hard."

"You'll just have to have faith that the good Lord will show you a way," Mother said with a deep sigh. "There'll come a day when Shannon will be thankful she has a fine brother like you." Mother smiled her sweet, sad smile and added, "You just wait and see."

Eleven: Pearl Harbor

Livy and me were in the kitchen cracking walnuts Sunday afternoon when we heard the news about Pearl Harbor. We just couldn't believe it for a while, but later when President Roosevelt made his speech to the nation, we had to accept it. We all expected the war to happen, but we didn't think we'd be attacked. I reckon the men over in Pearl Harbor weren't thinking about it either because hardly any of our planes got off the ground. In just two hours, we lost over two thousand men and had more than a thousand wounded.

Naturally, the first person I thought about was Buster. It didn't seem fair that a boy just four years older than me would get killed on the first day of the war, but I had an awful feeling in the pit of my stomach that something had happened to him.

Monday morning after Pearl Harbor I went to school feeling mighty low. Of course, I didn't know Buster was missing then, but I guess Mr. Vadas knew how confused all of us kids felt because he forgot Spanish that morning. He told us the war was going to be fought on the home front, too, and we were all soldiers. He said it was our duty to do whatever we could to help. He was in World War in 1918, and he said it was real important to the fighting men to know things were going on regular-like at home so their places would be ready for them when they got back.

He told us we'd have to go right on learning our lessons because those were our jobs for now. Then he asked if we'd like to do something extra to make folks at home feel better, especially with Christmas coming up. Naturally, we all said we would, so he told us his plan. We'd learn Christmas songs in Spanish and go caroling the week before vacation.

After we all agreed to the caroling he asked me to sing one of the songs he gave me before Thanksgiving. I guess everyone knows I'm a little shy, but when it comes to playing and singing I forget about it. So I just started right out singing "Noche de paz, noche de amor...." "Silent Night" is even prettier in Spanish than it is in English.

After that class I felt a little better. I knew there was only so much I could do, but I'd never thought about how important it was to keep up my own spirits and the ones of folks around me. But I didn't know then how hard that would be.

It seemed like everyone's nerves were on edge. After school that day, I could see that Derek Radcliffe was real upset. When Janet and I walked across the parking lot on our way home, Derek was standing by his car trying to get Shannon to get in. She was shaking her head as hard as she could, but Derek wasn't paying any attention to her.

We just stood there watching, hoping they'd get their problem worked out before we passed them. But when Derek grabbed Shannon's arm and tried to shove her into the car, I couldn't stand it any longer. "Maybe Shannon would rather walk home with us," I said, hurrying over to the car.

"Stay out of this, Sanford. This isn't any of your business," Derek yelled at me, but he didn't let go of Shannon's hand.

"Derek, what are you doing?" Janet yelled at her brother. "Leave Shannon alone." Janet walked up close and said, "Come on, Shannon, let's go home." Derek turned around to stare at his sister. He looked like he was ready to hit her, so I stepped up in front. When he saw me, I reckon it was just too much for him. He dropped Shannon's hand and threw a punch at me that would have flattened me if I hadn't stepped back and blocked his arm with a karate chop. He had a surprised look on his face for a second, and then it got red. If he'd been mad before, he was really mad now.

"You'll be sorry for this, Sanford," Derek yelled. Then he jumped in his car and slammed the door, and all three of us just stood there staring at him. The motor started on the first try, and Derek backed out without looking behind him. There was a loud crash as Derek plowed into a black Ford driving out of the parking lot.

In a second, Derek was out of the car yelling, "Why don't you watch where you're going, you damn fool!" He didn't realize who he'd hit until Coach Thompson jumped out of his car.

"Who are you calling a fool, young man? You backed into me. Look at that," he said, pointing at the caved-in door. "It's a good thing nobody was in the back seat. Now, give me your keys and get upstairs to Mr. Wallace's office." He took a second to catch his breath then added, "And you'd better call your father. There'll be some insurance papers to fill out."

For once, Derek didn't say a word. He just handed the coach his keys and started across the parking lot. Mr. Thompson watched Derek leave, then, he turned to us.

"What was going on here, anyway?"

Shannon looked like she was about to cry when she started talking, "Derek wanted me to go for a ride. He said he was going to enlist, and he wanted to talk about it. I told him I had to practice ballet, and he got mad."

"Why did he throw that punch at you, Seamus?"

"Well, I guess he was mad enough to hit someone, and I was handy," I answered.

The coach shook his head like he'd made up his mind about what to do and said, "You kids go on home. I'll park Derek's car and see if my old heap will move before I go to the office."

"Mr. Thompson, is Derek in a lot of trouble?" I asked. I didn't like Derek much, but I didn't want him to get kicked out of school over this.

"I wouldn't want to be in his shoes when his dad finds out what he's done. "And," he went on, "I expect Mr. Wallace will have a few choice things to say about all this."

We started down the street, not saying much at first. Shannon was still upset, and I didn't blame her. Finally she said, "Thanks for trying to help, Seamus. I don't know what's making him act so awful these days."

"I reckon it has something to do with the war. I heard one of his friends joined the Marines on Monday," I said.

"That was Blair Wright," Janet said. "He's failed so many classes he couldn't graduate anyway. He just stayed in school to play sports," Janet said.

"Right," Shannon agreed. "But Derek has already been offered a scholarship to Indiana State, so I haven't taken his talk about joining the navy seriously. He's mad at me because I've been practicing for the Christmas ballet and haven't had time to see him much."

"Well, that's selfish," I said.

By now, we'd reached Shannon's house, and she turned to say goodbye. She smiled a sad kind of smile and said, "Thanks a lot, you guys. I'm sure glad you were there."

We walked across the street to the Radcliffe house, and were talking when Janet's dad drove up and stopped in front. In a few seconds, her mom hurried outside and got in the car. When they saw us, Mrs. Radcliffe waved us over and asked what had happened at school. While Janet told them, her folks listened without saying a word.

When she finished the story, Mr. Radcliffe looked at me and said, "I can't believe he tried to hit you!"

"Well, he was awful mad. I reckon he wanted to hit Janet and me both, but I was in front of her."

After her folks drove off, I told Janet goodbye and jogged off home to start supper and do my homework.

The next day at school, everybody was surprised that Derek had been suspended a week for crashing into the coach's car and fighting on the school grounds. Nobody could believe the football captain and forward on the basketball team had done such a thing. But when he didn't show up at the basketball game with Martinsville, they knew it was true. Mr. Wallace didn't show any favoritism with Derek. He still had to do his schoolwork, but didn't get any credit for it. This close to the end of the semester, it sure wouldn't help his senior grade average.

Mr. Radcliffe was just as rough on him as the principal was. He made Derek go down to the Ford agency and help repair the coach's car, and he gave Mr. Thompson a car to use until his was fixed. I think the hardest thing for Derek was that he couldn't use his convertible for the rest of the semester.

All during that week we didn't see much of Derek. He went to work early and didn't come home until after five, so Shannon walked home with Janet and me.

It wasn't until the end of the week I heard Buster was missing in action at Pearl Harbor. Mother called me on the telephone to tell me she'd been over to see Mrs. Johnson right after she got the telegram about Buster. Mother's always there to help a neighbor in need, but a lot of folks don't feel that way about the Johnsons.

I didn't know exactly what missing in action meant. I wondered if the navy just couldn't find Buster or this was a warning that worse news was coming.

I couldn't understand why the news about Buster made me feel so bad. I hadn't even liked him much until he wrote and apologized for being such a butt head. Livy said it was probably because I'd never known anyone who'd died this young before, so it was a shock to know that young people died too. She told me not to give up hope since Buster could just be unaccounted for, not dead.

The week before vacation, it snowed and turned Marshall into a Christmas wonderland. I'd never lived in town before, so it was special to see the lights in the store windows and the ones folks hung on their porches.

I guess it must have been the snow or lights or something, but folks' spirits seemed to raise some, and they started doing Christmas shopping downtown. Nash's Radio Shop played carols on their loudspeakers, so I thought our Spanish songs would go over real well.

And I was right. We met the next afternoon in front of the courthouse and stood on the steps while we sang all six songs we'd learned. Since Mr. Vadas could sing real well and knew the words, we didn't get mixed up once. When we finished at the courthouse, we walked down Archer Avenue singing as we went. After we'd made a circuit of the business district and back to the Candy Kitchen, Edna came out and asked all fifteen of us to come in and have hot chocolate. By that time, we were really cold and glad to know that someone liked our singing enough to treat us to hot drinks.

The time before vacation went by real fast because we were all so busy. At school we had our regular work, and we had lots of war projects to do besides. Miss Greathouse got a list of the service men in Clark County, and she divided the names up so her typing students could write letters to them.

Usually at Christmas, she has her students write to faculty members, but she said it would be good for our men's morale to get letters from us. Since there was plenty going on in town, it wasn't hard to fill a page. I had to admit it was a lot more fun writing letters than typing exercises in the practice books.

Besides the regular Christmas program, we were having a school talent show to raise money for the Christmas packages we were sending to former high school students in the service. We assembled the packages and wrapped them at noon and after school. So, with all this going on besides our regular work, we didn't have much time to feel sorry for ourselves.

Of course, I still had my work to do around the Ashley place. The horses had to be exercised and groomed, but that was harder to do now that the days were so short. I wasn't upset when Mrs. Ashley wrote to say she'd made arrangements to have the horses sent to a big farm in southern Illinois before Christmas. She said they knew the war was likely to last a long time, and she didn't expect me to look after the horses that long. That meant I had to stay in Marshall until the horses were moved. Since Mrs. Ashley'd been so good about paying me, I didn't mind.

This was the first time I'd had my own money to buy Christmas presents, and I hadn't forgot about getting Mother and Dad a wind-up record player. I found one for $7.35, and since Livy paid for half of it, I had enough money to buy them three records besides the one I made for them.

By the time I'd finished my shopping, I didn't have much money left. I bought Livy a fountain pen and a pretty red cedar chest filled with stationery. After she used the paper it would make a nice box for jewelry or handkerchiefs. I was in a real quandary about what to buy Janet because I wanted it to be special. That's hard with no more money than I had.

Then our pictures taken for the high school annual came back, and that solved the problem. Janet asked me to save a picture for her, so I decided to buy a nice frame and have a photograph tinted down at Merrick's Studio.

It was the day before Christmas when the men from the horse farm came to get Blaze and Star. Until then, I'd been busy getting everything around the house ship-shape for Livy before I went home for a week. Livy made arrangements for Jimmy Black, who takes care of the Ashley's garden, to come over to fill the stoker and feed Duke and Stormy the two nights she'd be gone.

I could hardly wait to see Mother and Dad because I hadn't seen them since Thanksgiving. Dad met us in the pickup truck at Jones School two miles from home. He was worried about us because the weather had warmed up and the roads were so muddy he was afraid we'd get stuck. It was a good thing he did because Livy's little Ford mired down in the mud a mile from home. Coming home is always nice, but after all that had happened since I was here last, this time it was more special than ever.

Twelve: Buster Comes Home

You could have knocked me over with a feather when we heard Buster wasn't missing anymore. In fact, he knew where he was except for a couple days when he was in the hospital with a concussion. And the reason they couldn't find him was because he'd lost his dog tags. By the time he got his memory back, the telegram had already been sent to his mother.

I heard all this after I got home Christmas Eve, but it wasn't until five days later that I got a call from Buster. I couldn't believe he was calling from home, and wanted to come over to our house for a visit. I was mighty glad to know Buster was back, but I wondered how easy it would be to talk to him after all these years. I didn't have to wonder long because Buster was there before I knew it.

His brother, Jimmy Ray, drove up to the front gate and helped Buster out of his funny looking car. Jimmy Ray is quite a welder. He'd pieced the car together from a bunch of body parts he'd found in his dad's junkyard, so it was kind of a mongrel. He was drafted right after Thanksgiving, but he failed to pass his physical and is still hanging around home. He tried to hit me when I went to visit Mrs. Johnson last month. But since he was smiling today, I didn't think he remembered it.

"Howdy, Buster, " I said and walked down the front steps to meet him. He was on crutches because his left leg was in a cast up to his knee. "Watch that patch of ice on the sidewalk." When we got to the front door, Buster turned to wave at Jimmy Ray and said, "I'll call you when I want to come home."

I shut the front door and pulled a chair up close to the heating stove for Buster. Then I found a footstool to put under his leg. We didn't say much at first because it was hard to talk like friends after four years of not caring much for one another. Finally, Buster started talking.

"Thanks for the letter you wrote at Thanksgiving. It was the last letter I got before the attack," Buster said. "I wouldn't of blamed you if you hadn't wrote back."

"You apologized, so let's let bygones be bygones," I said, putting another shovel of coal in the stove to give me time to think of something to say next. "I reckon it's a sight cooler here than where you came from?"

"You can say that again. I wasn't there long, but Hawaii sure was pretty."

"I reckon so," I said, still trying to get the hang of talking to Buster. "How'd you get home so fast?"

"You'll never believe it," Buster grinned. "I'm a damned hero, that's why. I don't hardly remember it, but they said I pulled four guys out of the water and brought them to shore before a big piece of wreckage hit me. I felt it hit my head, but I didn't remember it hitting my leg."

"You mean they sent you home because you're a hero? Don't you ever have to go back to the ship?"

"Oh, yeah, when my leg gets well enough to climb back down in the engine room. They sent me and some other heroes home to sell war bonds." Buster laughed like he was enjoying the sound of the word, hero. "They put us on the first ship sailing for San Francisco with a bunch of civilians that wanted to get away from the war zone. I reckon they wanted to get us out of the hospital to make room for more. Besides we was too banged up to go back to the ships even if we had ships to go back to."

"Well, I'll be! How do you think you're going to like making speeches?"

"Making speeches! They didn't say nothin' about that. I figured I'd just kinda limp out after they introduced me and wave at everybody."

"That sounds too easy to me. I bet they'll expect you to tell 'em how you hauled all those guys out of the water." I had to grin to myself because the color left Buster's face the minute I mentioned him making speeches. "How'd you learn to swim so good?"

I could tell he was glad to be thinking about something besides making speeches. Buster grinned kind of sheepish-like and said, "I reckon I have Jimmy Ray to thank for that! He threw me in the Embarras River right after a big rain one spring. I must a' been about eight or nine at the time. I damned near drowned while I was learning to swim. And that dumb shit just stood on the bank laughing while I floundered in the muddy water."

"You mean he did it on purpose?"

"O' course he did. Sink or swim is what he said when he threw me in. An' he didn't care which way it went. When I finally climbed out like a half-drowned rat, scared to death and colder 'n a well-digger's butt, he said he was just teaching me to swim the way he learned."

"That's terrible. Did you tell your folks?"

"Naw, it wouldn't of helped. An' besides, he said he'd beat the shit out of me if I did. I reckon it did teach me something, though."

"What was that?"

"I'd better learn to swim real good while Jimmy Ray wasn't around in case he decided to give me another lesson," Buster laughed.

After hearing that story, I was beginning to feel sorry for Buster. With a brother like Jimmy Ray and a drunk for a father, it would of been a miracle if Buster'd had a sweet disposition.

We sat there not saying anything for a while, then I asked, "Say, Buster, were you scared when the Japs attacked?"

"You damned right I was scared. But lucky for me, I didn't have much time to think about it. I'd just come up on deck for a cigarette when I saw all the smoke and fire. At first I thought we'd been sabotaged," Buster said, catching his breath. "Our ships were anchored close together so it wouldn't take so many men to keep watch. I thought some ornery son of a bitch had set fire to 'em until I saw a dive bomber coming right at me."

"What did you do?"

"I hit the water fast. I reckon it's a good thing I did because a bomb hit the Tennessee next to us a few seconds later. Lucky for me, I was way down in the water, but I could still feel the vibrations."

"How'd you get back to the surface?"

"I swam like hell, kicking with all my might. When I shot up and took a big gulp of air, it was full of smoke. I went back down and stayed under water until I couldn't stand it no more."

"It must of been awful with all that smoke in the air." I broke in.

"You're not a kiddin'. When I looked back at the water, it was covered with burning oil from the damaged ships. I could see men trying to swim to shore, some of 'em on fire. It was so awful I could hardly stand to look." Buster's voice quivered. I could tell it really hurt him to talk about it.

"Well, how'd you get to be a hero?"

"After I got to shore I couldn't see much, but I could hear men yellin' for help. So when I'd spot one, I'd take a breath and swim out to get him. I reckon I did that three or four times until something hit me." He took a breath like he was remembering the awful scene. "After that, I didn't know what had happened until I woke up in the hospital."

"I don't think I could of done that," I said honestly.

"You never know for sure until it happens."

For a while neither of us said anything. I knew Buster was tired of talking about the attack, so we just sat there looking at the floor. I was sure glad when I saw Mother coming in with a lamp. Until then, I hadn't noticed that it was nearly dark.

"Well, I'll be! It's Buster Johnson," Mother said. "Why are you two sittin' here in the dark?" she asked as she put the lamp down on the library table. Buster tried to get up, but Mother told him to sit still and went over to shake hands with him. "I'm real glad to see you, and I know your mother is, too."

"I reckon so," Buster grinned at Mother. "She said you were mighty good to her when she thought I was missing."

"It's nothing any Christian wouldn't do," Mother said, but Buster and I both knew different. "Won't you stay to supper? I've plenty for one more." Mother gave the Aladdin lamp a final turn to adjust the flame and headed back to the kitchen. "Seamus, I'm going out to help Dad milk, so you just stay here and visit with Buster."

A little later I was throwing more coal on the fire when I heard a truck coming down the road, and we both looked up as we heard a door slam and someone hurry up the steps. Then I heard Mary Ruth Mason calling my name and opened the door.

"Hi, Seamus," she said giving me a quick hug, "Sorry I couldn't see you 'til now, but when Patty and John are home, everything around our house is crazy."

Mary Ruth hadn't seen Buster sitting on the other side of the heating stove. When she did, she looked kind of blank, like she didn't recognize him.

"You remember Buster Johnson, don't you? He's home on leave, and he's a certified hero," I said.

Mary Ruth stood next to me staring at Buster like she'd never seen him before. After a while she looked at me as if Buster wasn't there and said, "Well, his face has cleared up, and his hair is three shades lighter. I guess he's washed it and got a hair cut." Then she looked back at Buster again. He was trying to stand up. I wasn't sure if he was trying to be polite or to show her he'd slimmed down considerably. He didn't seem to know how to take her comments, but his face was flushed with excitement and he was smiling.

"And he's had his teeth fixed." She seemed to be finished with her review on Buster's improvements. Then she looked Buster straight in the eye and asked, "You hit any girls with rocks lately?"

Nobody said anything for a minute, but Mary Ruth didn't seem to notice while she settled down on the arm of my chair. I nudged her hoping she'd stop talking to Buster like that. But getting Mary Ruth to listen to something she doesn't want to hear is like getting a mule to move without a club.

"I was afraid you'd bring that up," Buster said. Then he ducked his head down to study the cast on his leg. "I'm real sorry about that."

"I bet! I can still feel that rock. Do you remember all the little kids you scared to death on the way home from school?"

If the room had been quiet before, it was deadly quiet now. Even the fire seemed to stop sputtering. "Mary Ruth, be quiet," I said. "Buster's sorry."

"How can you be so sweet after all the mean things he did to you?" With that last comment, Mary Ruth shut up. Nobody said a word until we heard Mother call out from the back door that she was back.

I knew Buster was just as relieved as I was when Mary Ruth jumped up and hurried into the kitchen. I could hear her asking Mother what she could do to help. Even with Mary Ruth out of the room, neither one of us could think of anything to say. So we just sat there like bumps on a log twiddling our thumbs.

Finally, Buster half stood up and said, "I think it's time I got home."

"But I thought you were staying for supper?"

"That was before Mary Ruth come," Buster blurted out. I'd never seen him look so shaky. "The navy may call me a hero, but after what she said, I'm not brave enough to eat supper with her. Not everyone's big enough to give a feller a second chance."

I knew he was right about Mary Ruth. She wasn't about to forgive him, at least not tonight. I didn't blame him for going home, so I went to the telephone and called his brother for him. Buster didn't want to wait inside by the fire for fear Mary Ruth would come in and ream him out again. So we both put on our coats and went out to the front gate to wait.

While we stood there with the winter wind whipping through our clothes, we kept our thoughts to ourselves. Then Buster finally said, "You know, Seamus. I didn't think I'd ever admit this to anyone, but I've always been sweet on Mary Ruth. I knew she thought I was lower than a snake's belly, and it pissed me off so I could hardly stand it. Then you come. Nothing but a scrawny little kid, and she liked you right off."

"I'm real sorry, Buster. I didn't know."

"You're quite a man, Seamus, learning to defend yourself instead of crying to the teacher."

In a few minutes, we heard Jimmy Ray's car bouncing over the ruts. The mud that had made the roads impassable a few days ago was frozen solid by the sub-zero temperatures. I helped Buster into the car. "Send me card now and then," I said. "Let me know how the speech-making goes."

Buster laughed and said he would, and Jimmy Ray gunned the motor as they took off in the early evening darkness.

After I helped Dad separate the milk, we went into the kitchen to wash for supper. Mother dished up her thick Irish stew and took the biscuits from the oven. Mary Ruth had set the table and was pouring coffee from the big blue coffee pot when we sat down to eat. She was humming and happy as could be.

Mary Ruth's real comfortable at our house even though it's pretty shabby compared to hers. She has a way of making herself at home wherever she is. I noticed this even when I was little. Now that I'm near grown, I wonder if it's because she knows who she is and is contented to be herself.

Mary Ruth's folks have a big farm and are college educated, and that's a rare thing in our part of the county. In spite of everything, Mary Ruth's never acted like she thought she was better than any of the other kids at school. Nobody seemed to resent her store-bought clothes even though ours were mostly homemade and hand-me-downs. She's always said exactly what was on her mind, and there have been times I've envied her style.

I'll never forget that first day at Jones school when I was in fifth grade. She seemed to take charge of me after Buster tried to take my new dinner bucket. She told me I could push her in the swing like she was doing me a big favor. Looking back, it might have been her way of letting the rest of the kids know that she liked me. Even though she was exasperating at times, she's been my best friend for a long time.

"Seamus," Mother asked me after we'd said grace, why didn't Buster stay to supper?"

"Oh, I guess he thought he ought go home to be with his mom. He'll be leaving soon." I didn't want to tell Mother the real reason, but naturally, Mary Ruth couldn't keep quiet.

"It was because of me, Mrs. Sanford. I couldn't stand that hero act. I just reminded him what a sh-, uh, what a jerk he was in grade school, and he couldn't take it. I bet he hasn't changed a bit on the inside, but I'll admit he looks a lot better." That was the end of Mary Ruth's comments for a while, and she turned her attention to the stew.

"Did Buster tell you about being at Pearl Harbor?" Dad asked, taking a sip of his coffee.

"Some, but I don't think he made it half as bad as it was. It seemed hard for him to talk about." I didn't feel like talking about it either, so I told Dad about Buster selling war bonds. "I reckon if he has to make speeches, it'll be harder than pulling those sailors out of the water."

Dad nodded and took another biscuit before he handed the plate to Mary Ruth. "So how's your brother these days? He going to stay in school?"

"My folks say he has to, but John wants to join up. He feels like a coward staying in college while the other boys are going to war."

"Yeah, but he does help your dad farm in the summer. As big as his farm is, he really needs John," Dad said.

"That's true. Mother's sure he'll never graduate if he quits now."

After we finished the stew, Mother got up to whip the cream for the applesauce cake, and I gathered up the plates.

While Mother served the cake, she told Mary Ruth about how I'd found the recipe for the Ozark Pudding. Naturally, Mary Ruth wanted to know if I'd found a secret compartment.

"I've looked at that desk a lot of times since then, but I haven't found a thing. It sure would be exciting if I found a hidden letter or something. I've heard that Mrs. Ashley's grandparents knew Abraham Lincoln, and he even came to supper there once," I said. "But that's probably just a family story."

"Interesting," Mary Ruth said. But I knew she'd heard plenty of Lincoln stories a lot closer to home. After all, we'd been brought up a few miles from the last Lincoln farm and Shiloh Cemetery, where his stepmother and father are buried.

After we finished supper, Mary Ruth started clearing the table while Mother finished her coffee. "I'll help Seamus with the dishes. Why don't you go and rest." I saw the flicker of a smile on Mother's lips as she looked up at Mary Ruth. It's the smile Mother gets on her face when she's pleased by something but doesn't want anyone to know. I knew she liked Mary Ruth a lot in spite of her sharp tongue.

Thirteen: Dark Days

January and February crept by slower than molasses. The days were busy enough, but the long nights gave me time to think about things I didn't want to. The war, mostly. It was hard to keep my spirits up when the Japanese were capturing places I'd only read about in geography books. Islands like Guam, Midway and Wake. The President ordered General MacArthur to leave the Philippines and go to the Bataan Peninsula. Then, on March 11, he had to go to Australia. When MacArthur said, "I shall return," I wondered if he ever would.

I reckon I was discouraged because this was the first time I'd experienced winter and war at the same time. I really didn't understand any of it, the fighting and killing. It seemed like it was all because a couple bullies wanted more than their share of land. Everything seemed worse because it was cold! And winter in Illinois is hard enough when things are going right.

But suddenly, a miracle happened. Oh, I guess it wasn't really anything different. But this year it seemed extra special.

Spring had finally come!

Even folks who'd had the gloomiest faces all winter lightened up a little. It's pretty hard to be sad when the first robin comes home to build a nest. Or you see violets and daffodils and periwinkle popping up everywhere. The real miracle is when you see early flowers blooming right next to a snow bank. It's like they couldn't wait to spread good cheer and to remind Old Man Winter he'd overstayed his welcome.

Spring is the time to change out of long underwear. That almost beats the flowers as a sign of spring. I used to wonder if the girls at Jones School were glad when they didn't have to wear ugly long stockings that bagged at the knees. Naturally I was too polite to ask how they felt when they started wearing anklets again.

While we were eating supper that Friday night, I asked Livy, "Do you think Mother's out digging for sassafras yet?"

"What on earth made you think about that?" Livy asked. We were eating the last of the strong-tasting winter turnips, and I was wishing for some fresh greens.

"Oh, about this time of the year, I'm hungry for something that isn't dried or canned. You know, like new lettuce 'n radishes 'n little green onions."

"Well, I think the best you can hope for right now would be dandelion greens. It looks like we have a good crop growing out in the back yard." Livy laughed and said she'd make the salad if I'd dig 'em up.

"How would it taste without onions and those other things you put in salads?" I asked. I wasn't sure she was serious about picking dandelions to eat.

"I guess it would depend on how hungry you are for greens. There's an old tumbled-down cabin back in that grove of trees in the pasture, and Mrs. Ashley said the homesteaders who built it had an herb garden. I noticed it's spread all over the pasture. We might go back there and see if there are any potherbs."

"How would we know we weren't digging up something poison?"

"Well, I want you to know, your sister studied something in college besides English. I had a class in botany, and I still have Gray's Manual and my illustrated notebook that Dr. Thut gave me an A on. I can identify things like sheep sorrel, poke, dock, lamb's quarters and mustard. Want to go look tomorrow?"

"Sure. I didn't know about the cabin, but I did notice a little stream back there. There's always a trickle of water in it."

"That's because there's a spring that feeds it. It's probably the reason the pioneers settled there. We'll go exploring after we get the sassafras. That's where I saw the tree, back by the brook."

"Are you serious about getting the sassafras? That would be fun," I said. "Do you really think we need our blood thinned in the spring like Mother says?"

Livy thought for a moment before she answered. "I'm not about to question Mother's theories. It's probably as much folklore as fact, but I always enjoyed a cup of sassafras tea in the spring. It seemed by drinking it, we gave winter a shove and did something to welcome spring."

"Are you laughing at me, Livy?"

"Of course not. It's wonderful to see you excited about something. I guess drinking sassafras tea in the spring is kind of like believing in the Easter Bunny or the Tooth Fairy."

I got up to pour Livy more coffee, but there were only a few drops left. "Looks like we're out of coffee," I said. "I've been hearing that the government's talking about rationing coffee and sugar, and I bet some folks are hoarding it right now."

"No doubt. Rationing can't be far off, so I think I'll make a batch of cookies while I still have sugar," Livy said, kind of defiant-like. "Why don't you get some of your friends to help dig sassafras, and we'll have a tea party Sunday afternoon?"

Livy couldn't have said anything to make me feel better. So right after we did the dishes, I called Scooter. Nobody can have a party without inviting Scooter, even though it's just sassafras tea and cookies.

"You're kidding!" Scooter laughed after I'd told him about the party. "You really going to drink tea made from tree roots?"

"Yeah, but we'll have something else in case you don't like it. Anyway, it's a good excuse to get together. You can bring some records." Naturally, he said a few more dumb things about sassafras tea, but he said he'd come.

After I hung up, I called Janet and asked her. I'd walked home with her after school all winter, but we didn't do much but go to a movie or to the Candy Kitchen once in a while. I could tell she was excited.

"Are you going to call Shannon?" Janet asked. "She hasn't been seeing much of my brother lately, and I bet she'd like to come."

"Sure, and I'll ask the judge. I haven't seen him in ages." I knew he was busy with court cases, and he was on the draft board, too. I figured it wasn't easy to send men to war, especially ones he'd known most of his life.

That Sunday afternoon, it was a strange looking bunch of people that set out across the pasture to dig roots from the sassafras tree. Livy had told everyone to wear old shoes and everyday clothes, and they were surprised when she gave us baskets and buckets to take along. She brought a shovel and a knife to dig up the tender roots of the sassafras, but she didn't tell us until we got to the tree what we were supposed to put in the baskets.

"I'm going to give you a short lesson in gathering herbs," Livy told us, taking Gray's Manual out of her basket. "There are all kinds of edible greens out here, so I want you to start looking for plants likes these." Everyone gathered around Livy while she showed us pictures of the plants she wanted us to find. "Scooter, you and Janet look for wild onions,"

Livy handed him a gardening trowel and told them to look at the picture again. "Look for a small plant with grass-like leaves and white or rose-colored flowers like these," she pointed to the plant in the book. "You'll recognize it by the onion-like smell," she added before they set off.

Then she told Shannon and me to dig for watercress over by the brook. She read to us from the book, "The stems grow up to ten inches tall. They have dark green leaves that look scalloped and have a pungent taste and smell." After we looked at the picture again, she and the judge started digging for roots at the sassafras tree. The judge seemed pleased to be a part of this, and I could tell he was having a good time. He didn't say a word about how dumb it was to be digging up weeds and roots. With all the hard decisions he had to make all week, I reckon this was easy work.

At first, we didn't hear anything from anyone, then Janet squealed and said, "Oh, look at this, Scooter. These onions are all over the place."

After a while Shannon and I started finding patches of watercress, and she said it was almost like looking for Easter eggs. When we had filled our baskets, Livy sent all of us to look for pokeweeds, mustard and lamb's quarters. After an hour or so,

Livy finally said, "We've gathered enough greens for threshers, so let's go back to the house and have tea."

When we finished our work, our shoes were muddy, and our clothes had leaves and dirt stuck to them. Shannon had slid down the side of the brook and got her jeans muddy. I'd never seen her looking messy before, but she seemed more, well, more human. Her eyes sparkled, and she looked happy and excited. I remembered the first time I saw her when I was cleaning the stable. She looked pretty then, but today with her hair blowing loose, she looked even prettier.

We all took off our muddy shoes before traipsing into the kitchen. It was nice and warm, and it felt real homey with the steam coming out of the teakettle. Livy sent us to the bathrooms to wash up a bit, then we came back to sit around the kitchen table.

While we were gone Livy had boiled the sassafras roots and put the tea into one of Mrs. Ashley's silver teapots. She'd put the cookies on a glass plate and had little cream cheese sandwiches topped with watercress.

Everything looked real festive with the sliver teapot, linen napkins and China cups and saucers. The sassafras tea smelled real nice as she poured it into the delicate cups. It reminded me of the time I went to the Daughter's of American Revolution tea after my essay won the American History Essay Contest back in the eighth grade.

It was fun to watch folks' expressions when they took the first swallow. Shannon took a sip, looked surprised and said, "I didn't think it would be this good." Janet nodded in agreement. I didn't say anything because I was watching Scooter making faces as he sniffed the tea.

Then he took a swallow and said, "I sure hope one cup is enough to purge my blood, because that's all my body can stand." Everyone laughed as he put down his cup and wiped his mouth on a linen napkin.

"Here," Livy said, handing him a tray of cookies, "try my homemade gingersnaps." Scooter took a cookie and passed them around the table. Then Livy handed him the tray of little sandwiches before she poured more tea.

While we sipped our tea and ate, Livy told us some things about sassafras. "It was used to cure all kinds of ailments from lung fevers to skin trouble. There was even a song to advertise it." Then she sang the words. "'In the spring of the year when the blood is too thick, there is nothing so fine as a sassafras stick.'"

We all laughed at Livy's singing, then Shannon asked. "Did you learn this in botany?"

"Well, not really," Livy smiled and nodded her head like she was pleased that Shannon was enjoying herself. "I first got interested in botany when I was a girl and visited a neighbor named Bessie Beals. In the spring the two of us had tea parties just like this. Almost everyone thought she was touched in the head because she gathered herbs all over the county."

"Did they think she was a witch?" Shannon asked.

"No, but they did think she was pretty strange. What they didn't know was that she made a good living gathering plants for a big pharmaceutical company in Chicago."

"She must have gotten a big laugh from that," Shannon smiled. "Would you show me how to make a little herb garden in our back yard this summer?"

"I'd be glad to. But it'll have to be after my classes at Indiana State," Livy said.

"What are you taking, Olivia?" Judge Williams seemed surprised by this, and I was, too since she hadn't mentioned it to me.

"I'm starting my doctorate program," Livy answered. With Seamus back on the farm helping Dad, I want to keep busy this summer."

"Oh, I didn't know you'd be going back home," Janet said. I was glad she looked sad about it. "What will you do?"

"By the time I get home, Dad will have the crops planted, but there'll be plenty of weeds to plow. I'll be driving the tractor from early light 'til dark."

"Do you like to do that?" Shannon asked.

"I don't mind, but it gets a little boring after a while."

"I bet it isn't any worse than working in a print shop," Scooter broke in, "and I expect dust is easier to wash off than printer's ink."

"Your dad used to complain about that when we were kids," the judge laughed. "He envied me because I hung around my dad's law office doing errands and answering the telephone. What he didn't know was my dad was trying to get me interested in law so I'd follow the family tradition."

"I reckon it worked," I laughed, "and now you're a judge like your father.

We sat around the kitchen table laughing and talking a long time, and finally Janet asked Livy what she was going to do with all the plants we gathered and washed.

"Seamus is hungry for fresh greens," Livy smiled, "so I'm going to make a big salad to serve with the wieners we're going to roast for supper. I've already made the potato salad."

"Oh," Janet said, "that sounds like fun."

"It will be," Livy said, laughing and gathering up the dishes. "Why don't you kids go into the living room and listen to records. I'll put together a salad big enough for six hungry people."

Shannon and Janet went into the living room with Scooter, but the judge put his hand on my shoulder and said, "I'm really glad to see Shannon looking so much happier these days. Have you noticed the change?"

"Yeah, she does seem more interested in what everyone else is doing. Do you think she's beginning to get over her mother's death?"

"I hope so, and I'm pleased she's not spending so much time with Derek. I've been worried about him. I think he's drinking these days, and I'm afraid his folks aren't aware of it."

I started to say something, but I heard Janet calling me from the living room. The judge told me to go on and have fun and he'd help Livy in the kitchen. When I went in, Shannon was telling Scooter it was time he learned to dance. He complained that he had two left feet, but Shannon wouldn't listen to his excuses.

"Besides," Scooter said, trying to finish his sentence, "I'm shorter than all the girls I'd dance with."

"Turn around, Scooter, and stand next to Shannon," Janet told him, putting her hand on their heads. "See, you're just as tall as she is. Now will you shut up and let her show you how to jitterbug?"

It turned out that Scooter's feet weren't very well matched to do the jitterbug, but after a while he did learn the two-step. Shannon and Janet both told him they weren't giving up on him, and I think he was glad to have two of the prettiest girls in school paying so much attention to him.

That afternoon was the most fun I'd had in a coon's age, and I knew everyone else felt the same way. I wasn't sure if the sassafras tea had done the trick or it was because spring had finally come.

All winter I'd been doing my schoolwork in the kitchen because it was warm, instead of at the desk in Mrs. Ashley's office where I'd studied until cold weather. Now it was piled high with my stuff. Before

I could use the desk again, I had to put everything away. I took out the little drawers on top of the desk to organize and clean them. I arranged pencils in one, and put note cards, paper clips and other stuff in the others.

That's when I noticed something strange about one drawer, so I turned it over to look at the bottom. Then I looked at it again from the front. That's when I realized the outside of the drawer was just as deep as the others, but there was only half the depth on the inside. I didn't know what to make of it, so I turned it around again and looked at the back. A rusty hook was latched over a tiny nail that held the bottom in place. Once I pried the hook up with my pocketknife, I slid the bottom right out. The drawer was divided horizontally into two parts, making a secret compartment in the bottom.

That's where I found the old letter!

Springfield, Ills.

August 1, 1850

My dear Madam
This note of thanks is long overdue--but I beg your understanding. Mary has reminded me a second time to thank you for the hospitality you and the colonel showed me last month. After leaving Marshall I spent several days

in Charleston, where I had some legal work, and also visited my aged mother.

If your fine meal is an example of the quality of cooking in Marshall--you must be the best cook in town. Since my return, Mary has made your Ozark Pudding several times, and she thanks you for the recipe. It has received high praise from our Springfield friends.

Yours very truly,

A. Lincoln

I couldn't believe what I was seeing. Could Lincoln have been talking about the recipe I found last fall? If so, where had it come from? I'd probably never know unless the old desk suddenly started talking.

For a while I sat there reading the note, then my hands started shaking. I didn't even remember yelling for Livy until I felt her touch my arm.

"What's going on, Shamie? You look like you've seen a ghost."

"Look what I found in this secret drawer."

"Secret drawer!" Livy exclaimed in surprise. She looked at the drawer for a second before taking the letter from my cold fingers. After she read it, she didn't say anything for a while. Finally she said, "It looks real, and I'm sure it's old."

"Yeah, and if it's genuine, it's valuable. Should we call the judge? His wife was Mrs. Ashley's niece."

"I know. And her son is the president of the bank. But I've only met him a few times." Livy looked a little uncertain about what to do.

We thought about what to do for a while, and then I said, "Let's get your camera and take pictures of the letter and the envelope and the secret drawer. We can send the film to Mrs. Ashley and let her decide what to do."

"I guess you're right," Livy agreed. "When we're finished, we'll put the letter back in the drawer and wait 'til we hear from her. After all, it's been there nearly a hundred years. The fewer people who know about it, the safer it will be."

Livy handed the letter back to me, and I looked at it again. "You know these dashes he used instead of commas," I said, pointing to the dashes."

"What about them?"

"Well, after I gave my Lincoln report in history last semester, my teacher brought in some books that showed a bunch of Lincoln's letters. Mr. Singer explained that Lincoln liked to punctuate with dashes, but after he was elected President his secretaries changed a lot of things to make them more correct. I'd think a note like this would be real valuable."

"You're probably right," Livy said. "I'll get my camera."

After taking a whole roll of film I typed an exact copy of the letter before putting it back in the drawer. I planned to send everything to Mrs. Ashley in Washington right away. Then I wrote a letter and explained about finding the Lincoln note in a secret drawer of her desk, and I also asked if she'd give the first shot at the story to Scooter if the letter turned out to be real.

Wouldn't he be proud to write that story for his dad's paper?

The Red Headed Girl

Fourteen: Mother Meets Shannon

Since the first of April, I've been going home every weekend to help Dad with the farming. Stock and grain prices are better than ever, and it looks like farmers will have to produce a lot to feed our country at war.

Even though things are fine on the farm, the war's not going well for us. The first good news came on April 18 when Lt. Col. Jimmy Doolittle and sixteen B-25 planes bombed Tokyo. It wasn't a big victory, but it made us Americans feel better. The newspapers called it a morale booster.

At school, the kids are looking forward to vacation. A lot of them have summer jobs lined up. There's a manpower shortage because so many men have been drafted or joined the service on their own. Some of the senior boys have volunteered, and I think they're hoping to get called up before final exams. Janet says Derek is still acting weird, but she doesn't know if it's because he can't decide to join up or that Shannon doesn't come running every time he calls.

Track season started as usual, but I didn't try out for it. Most of the meets take place on Fridays, and I leave school early to catch the Greyhound bus to Greenup. This week when I got off the bus in front of Peg's Diner, Mary Ruth Mason was waiting for me.

"Hi, Seamus," she grinned. "Are you surprised to see me?"

"Yeah. How did you know I was coming?"

"Your mother. She invited me to come for supper, so I couldn't say no," Mary Ruth laughed.

"That's nice," I said, picking up my bag the bus driver had just set on the sidewalk. I suddenly realized she was leaning against a new convertible, and she had a silly grin on her face. It took me a minute to figure it out, but finally I did. "Hey, is this your car?"

"Yeah."

"Are you kidding? When did you get it?"

"Uncle Ray got it in last week, but he didn't even put it in his showroom. He talked Daddy into buying it for me. He said it would be the last new car he'd get until after the war."

"What did your dad say when he gave it to you?"

"He told me he'd bought it because I'd been on the honor roll for three years, but I think the real reason is that he doesn't like the way I drive his truck." She laughed and got into the driver's seat.

"Your dad has spoiled you rotten," I said, looking at the bright blue convertible. It smelled like new leather, and I couldn't help being a little jealous. I wondered if Mary Ruth knew how lucky she was to have a brand new car at sixteen.

"When we get off the slab, I'll let you drive," she said, as she backed out of the parking place.

"Really? But I don't have a driver's license."

"So what, you've been driving since your legs were long enough to reach the pedals. It's a lot easier to drive than your dad's International truck." I knew she was right about that, because that truck drives about as hard as the tractor.

On the way to Toledo, Mary Ruth told me about the dress Mother was making for her. "Since I knew I could only have one new formal this spring, I got a pattern I really liked. My mother said it was too complicated for her, so I asked your mom."

"Since she doesn't have anything else to do," I said. I knew it must have sounded sarcastic, but it went right over Mary Ruth's head. "So why would you want more than one new dress?"

"Well, my brother invited me to his fraternity dance, and I couldn't go in the kind of dress I'd wear to the junior-senior banquet at Toledo."

"I can't believe you'd want to go to John's dance," I said.

"Well, there are a lot of cute guys in the Sigma Nu, and John said this would probably be the last dance until after the war," she laughed. "I thought I'd better go while I had a chance."

"So, how's this dress going to work for the fraternity dance and the banquet?" Sometimes it's hard to follow Mary Ruth's mind when it really starts rolling.

"The dress is strapless, but it has a little bolero. With the jacket, I can wear it to the banquet, but I can take it off and look very sophisticated at the frat dance." I thought she was finished, but she went on to explain that Mother called to tell her the dress was ready for a fitting. That's when Mary Ruth volunteered to meet me at the bus.

By the time she'd finished telling me about her dress, we were on the gravel road outside of Toledo. She stopped so I could get in the driver's seat.

Even though we were on a country road and nobody could see me, I felt like a big "butter 'n egg man" sitting behind the wheel of that car.

She looked over at me and grinned like she knew what I was thinking as I put the car in gear and started down the road. "It feels good, doesn't it?" Mary Ruth said.

I nodded my head, but it wasn't just driving the car that made me happy. It was a wonderful spring afternoon, and it was nice to be with my best friend, even though sometimes she sounds like a scatterbrain.

I didn't drive very fast because of the rough road. Even in the new Chevy, the road felt like I was driving over a washboard. For a while we were quiet, then Mary Ruth surprised me by asking if I'd heard from Buster lately.

"Yeah, I got a letter after his bond-selling trip. He said he'd seen a lot of country, but he didn't say anything about his ship. They're not supposed to tell folks where they are or what they're doing for fear the information could fall into enemy hands."

"I could hardly believe it when I got a letter from him," she said. "He wrote to apologize for hitting me with that rock back in grade school. Remember how obnoxious he was that day when I walked home from school with you? That was the day you threw him in the muddy ditch?"

"I sure do, and him yelling all that stuff about orphans being so dumb. It made me feel awful. Back then, I thought I was a bastard, that is, I thought my folks weren't married," I laughed, forgetting I didn't need to be careful what I said in front of Mary Ruth.

"Do you know what he said about that rock?"

"I can't even guess."

"He said he was trying to hit you, not me. Now isn't that something to apologize for?" Mary Ruth's laugh was kind of sinister, like she'd yank Buster's hair out by the roots if she could get her hands on him. "Can you believe that! Apologizing for being a lousy shot. I'm a little worried about our country with Buster on our side."

I had to laugh at Mary Ruth, but at least Buster was down in the engine room, not up on deck where he might hit our men instead of the Japanese.

I didn't waste much more time thinking about Buster though. It was such a wonderful day, and I was thrilled to be behind the wheel of Mary Ruth's new car. I'd never even been in a convertible before let alone drive one. I was really having a good time as I turned east on the Bradbury road past the Mason's house, Jones School and all my friends' houses along the way. I honked and waved at everyone we passed.

When we got home, Mother was coming in from the chicken house with a basket of eggs, and Bobbie was at her heels. I hurried around to the back porch where she was waiting for me.

"I'm sure glad to see you, son," Mother said, giving me a hug. She looked around and asked, "Where's Mary Ruth?"

"Putting up the top of her car," I said, leaning down to pet Bobbie. She'd been barking like crazy ever since she saw me, and I was glad she hadn't forgotten me.

Before I went out to do the chores I put on my faded overalls and straw hat and went to get the cows. It felt good to be home, and I was glad just to be me. This last year living with Livy, I wasn't always sure who I was. I wasn't used to being with people with education and money. Even after driving Mary Ruth's new car, I was still glad to be plain old Seamus Sanford doing chores. Since Dad was still working in the field, I was going to do the milking tonight.

Milking twelve Jersey cows isn't such a chore now that Dad has milking machines. We still don't have electricity, but a gasoline motor powers the machines. All I have to do is strip the last bit of milk from the cow after I unhook the machines. This was the first time I'd done the milking all by myself, but the cows cooperated just fine. They didn't seem to notice I wasn't Dad.

By the time I'd finished the milking, Dad was home. He was out on the porch trying to get the field dust off with a wash pan full of water. It was a good thing mother had sent him outside because he'd splashed water everywhere.

That night we had a good supper starting with spring lettuce that was real tart and tasty. Mother had fried bacon and added vinegar and sugar to the warm grease as a salad dressing. Wilted lettuce is a big favorite of mine. That's what made me think of telling them about gathering the early greens at our sassafras tea party back in March.

When I mentioned Shannon, Mary Ruth broke in. "So when are we going to get to see your stuck-up sister?"

I didn't know if she was serious about wanting to see Shannon or not, but she hasn't formed a very high opinion of my twin. Mary Ruth doesn't understand why I haven't told Shannon I'm her brother before now. She thinks everyone should be glad to have a brother like me.

"Livy's going to bring Shannon and the judge over Sunday to pick me up."

"Well, for goodness sakes," Mother said before I could finish. "She should have told me. I'll just call Olivia and have them come for Sunday dinner." I knew Mother had wanted to meet Shannon for a long time, but I wasn't sure I'd want to have Mary Ruth around. I like her a whole lot, but she says whatever comes to mind and never thinks first.

Lucky for me, Mary Ruth's mind flits from one subject to the next at the speed of light. Since her mind was now on the dress Mother was making for her, she didn't ask any more questions about Shannon. I guess Mother was anxious to see how the dress fit, so as soon as we finished supper, they went into the bedroom and left me to do the dishes.

Saturday morning Mother woke me early so I could get to the field by sunup. She fixed me a big lunch, and I filled a gallon jug with water. Dad had wrapped several layers of burlap around it and tied it on with binder twine. I soaked the burlap with water to help keep it cool. Mother warned me not to leave my shirt off very long because I sunburn real fast in the spring. Even though I'm six feet tall and will be fifteen in August, she still thinks I'm just a kid.

When I got to the hill that overlooks the river, I could see the first rays of the sun slanting through the trees. Down below in the river bottom, new crops were just peeping through the black soil, rich and fertile with silt from the Embarras River. I never get tired of looking at the acres and acres of good land that Dad and our neighbors cultivate. In a distant field I could see a tractor on the Camwell land kicking up dust. There aren't any fences around these fields since they're not used for pasture, but narrow roads for farm machinery separate them. Before I headed to our land, I drove over to the river and put my lunch under a tree where it would stay cool.

I had a lot to think about this morning. With Shannon and the judge coming for the first time, I wondered what they'd think of the way we live. Our house is little and mighty common compared to the judge's big, brick place. His is a Victorian and has lots of fancy white trim on the outside, and it has a bathroom upstairs and downstairs, too. I'm not ashamed of being a poor farmer's son. In fact, I'm mighty proud. Being away in Marshall, living in the Ashley's mansion has made me look at our place in a new light.

While I plowed weeds out of row after row of new corn, I thought about Shannon. She's not an easy girl to get to know, but I reckon that's natural since we've been raised by parents with different backgrounds. Now that I've finally stopped trying to understand her, I think she's more shy than stuck-up.

Sunday morning when I woke up I could hear the folks on the porch, Dad's voice raised over the noise of the cream separator. Since he's a little hard of hearing, he talks louder than most folks do.

"Now, Hannah, stop worrying about your dinner. I've never had a bad meal at your table even if it was cornbread and milk. Your fried chicken is the best there is."

"But I don't have any good dishes or silver, and they're used to fine things," Mother said wistfully.

"You've never mentioned you wanted those things before," Dad said, puffing a little from turning the separator. "We have enough money for a new set of dishes. I saw some in the catalog for less than ten dollars."

"How'd you know that?" Mother asked.

"I noticed you had the page turned down, and you'd added the cost of the set of Roger's silver plate, and both sets only come to twenty-three dollars."

Mother laughed, "I didn't think you ever looked at anything in the catalog but harness and farm machinery."

Since I didn't want the folks to know I'd been listening to them, I hurried to dress and was standing by the cook stove pouring my coffee when they came into the kitchen.

"Morning, Seamus," Mother said, pecking my cheek as she walked by. "What time do you reckon Olivia will get here?"

"Oh, I expect she'll wait 'til we get home from Sunday school," I said, helping myself to the breakfast Mother'd set out for me. "What do you want me to do to help?" I asked. Mother poured herself a cup of coffee and we sat down at the kitchen table piled high with flowers. It looked like she was getting ready for a flower show. But then, Mother never does anything by halves. She'd already arranged a bouquet of jonquils in a green glass vase I bought her at the dime store when I was ten. There were more flowers in a bucket of water waiting to be put in vases.

"You can help me catch some young roosters and bring in water to heat so I can scald them," Mother said. Then she looked at the clock and added, "I'd like to have the chickens browned and in the oven before we go to church."

Mother kept me busy plucking feathers and doing other stuff, but I could tell she was happy getting ready for company. She didn't mention not having new dishes and silverware. I was ashamed I didn't even know she wanted them. Before we set the table, I put in an extra leaf, and Mother got out her hand-embroidered tablecloth and napkins. With the big bouquet of flowers in the middle of the table, I thought it looked festive even though the dishes didn't match.

We hadn't been home from church long when the judge's big Buick stopped in front. We all went out to meet them like folks do on the farm. Livy introduced Mother and Dad to the judge and Shannon, and then everyone but me and Shannon went inside. She couldn't make out why my folks seemed so happy to see her.

At first Shannon seemed awful shy. Then Bobbie came out to see what all the commotion was about and started dancing around on her back feet. Shannon laughed and petted Bobbie and sat down to shake hands. "What a sweet little dog," Shannon said, shaking Bobbie's paw.

I decided to show Shannon around the farm while my folks got acquainted with the judge. I figured they'd have a lot to talk about. I called to Mother that we were going to the river, and we walked down the lane to the big hay barn. We stopped at the gate that leads down to the river.

"This is where the river starts to bend in the shape of a big horseshoe, then it turns again about a mile down the road," I said, pointing toward the river.

"So that's why this area is called the Bend?"

"Yeah, and that's where we farm." I opened the gate and we went through. "Be careful going down the hill," I said and took hold of Shannon's arm where the hill's real steep. I never walk down it that I don't think of the time I slid all the way down on the seat of my pants. That was the day I sang at the fish fry picnic when I was ten. When I told Shannon about it, she laughed so hard she almost fell herself.

"You're so funny, Seamus. You seem different here."

"Well, I may be. I love this farm, but I like living with Livy in Marshall, too." By this time we were down the hill near the river, and there's a nice slanting bank to the water's edge. I picked up a flat rock and skipped it three times before it sank into the water.

"I bet I can do better than that," Shannon laughed as she searched for a flat rock. She leaned down and took careful aim, and the rock skimmed over the water four times before it disappeared. Shannon looked pleased with herself, but she didn't brag about beating me. We stood there skipping rocks for a while without saying anything. Then she finally looked at me and said, "This sure is a pretty place. Do you swim here?"

"Yeah, this is where I learned. We don't have much time to swim just for fun, but Dad and I take baths here from the time it gets warm enough until cool weather."

"Oh," she said in surprise, "I guess you don't have a bathroom. I bet that's a real pain in winter."

"Yeah, but we manage," I said, not much wanting to talk about the rest of the bathroom situation, so I changed the subject. "Do you want to go see the kittens before we go back to the house?"

"Oh, yes," Shannon said. "How old are they?"

"They're six weeks old now, big enough to play and explore. The mother is a calico, so I call her Callie. She's Stormy's mother. You know, the cat I brought to Marshall."

"Yes, I remember. She's beautiful."

On the way up to the barn we talked about the cats we'd had, and by the time we got there, I knew

Shannon liked cats as much as I do. I opened the wide barn doors so we could see well enough to get up into the haymow.

"We have to climb up in the mow to see the kittens because Callie seems to know the they're safer up there." I went up first and helped Shannon into the mow and over the bale of hay that kept the kittens in their hiding place. It was a little darker in the loft, but the big opening where the hay is hauled into the barn let in enough light to see.

"Oh, look at those kittens," Shannon said, scrambling down between two bales where the pile of sleeping kittens lay in a nest of loose hay. "How many are there?"

"Four," I said, sitting down on the floor to pick up the white one. "Here's one that looks like Stormy. She's all white."

As I gave Shannon the kitten, it opened its eyes and meowed. That woke the others and they started mewing and searching for dinner. Shannon sat down by me and cuddled the white kitten next to her cheek without saying anything. After a while, she looked down at the other kittens. "That's funny, they're all different. I wonder how she came to have just one white kitten."

"Well," I laughed. "There's a big white Tom that lives in the cow barn, so I guess this kitten takes after its daddy."

Shannon held the kitten up to look at her more closely and started talking to her. "I'd like to take you home with me." Then she looked at me and asked, "Is she old enough to leave her mother?"

"Yeah, they must be nearly six weeks old by now," I said, picking up a calico kitten. "They're old enough now to drink milk from a pan. Do you think your dad would let you have one?"

"Oh, Daddy wouldn't care. She'd be a lot of company," Shannon sighed sadly. "Sometimes I get so lonely." She kind of left the sentence unfinished, but I knew she was thinking about her mother.

We sat there playing with the kittens for a while, taking turns holding them all. But I noticed Shannon didn't put the white kitten down long before she picked it up again. There isn't anything sweeter than a baby kitten, and I was glad to know my sister felt the way I did. After a while, I heard Livy calling that it was time to eat.

Shannon started to put the kitten down, but changed her mind. "I'm sure Daddy wouldn't mind, and if you don't care, I'd love to take this kitten home."

"I knew you were going to say that," I laughed and started down the ladder. "I'll go down first and you can hand her to me," I said. When I was nearly down, Shannon gave me the kitten. The movement scared her, so I let her get her claws into my shirt and held her close. After Shannon got down, she took the kitten and we headed up to the house.

When we came into the kitchen, Mother looked at Shannon and the kitten. "Just like Seamus," she laughed, "He can't leave the kittens in the barn where they belong." Are you taking that little one home with you?"

"If you don't mind," Shannon answered, holding the kitten up for Mother to see. "Seamus said this kitten's Stormy's sister."

"I can't keep track of all our cat families, but I'm sure Seamus knows," Mother said. The judge looked at Shannon and the kitten, then over at me. He nodded his head and smiled like he was real pleased about something. I knew he was glad to see Shannon happy and that we were having a good time together.

Livy came into the kitchen and saw the kitten Shannon was holding and said, "It looks like another of Callie's kittens is going to Marshall. I'll find a flower sack for her to sleep on, and you can put her in Mother's egg basket until we go."

Mother was trying to take up dinner and wanted us out of her way. "Now, you young'uns go wash your hands. It's time to eat." I pumped some water in the wash pan for Shannon, and we washed our hands and took the kitten into the living room where it was quiet.

The meal was one of Mother's best with fried chicken, mashed potatoes and gravy and another wilted lettuce salad. Naturally, we had hot rolls and butter, and then we had angel food cake for dessert. While we ate, there was a lot of easy small talk, and I could tell the judge liked my folks, and they liked him. It was a nice feeling to have folks I loved to like each other. Mother did her share of talking, but all through the meal, I noticed she kept glancing at Shannon, then over at me. I knew what she was thinking because it hadn't been quite five years since the Rawleigh man had been sitting right here eating with us. That's when he told me about the redheaded girl.

The Red Headed Girl

Fifteen: The Stable Burns

On the drive home to Marshall Sunday afternoon, Shannon and I tried to think of a name for her kitten. At first she thought Cinderella would be nice. But after she said it a few times, she decided Cindy fit the kitten a lot better.

Cindy slept most of the way even though we were singing silly songs like "The Three Little Fishies" and "The Woodpecker Song." But when we started doing the clapping part to "Deep in the Heart of Texas," Cindy woke up." I guess she must have been hungry because she cried the rest of the way to Marshall. We were all glad when the judge pulled up in front of the house, and we could get out of the car. Since I knew a hungry kitten when I heard one, I hurried inside to get Cindy some milk.

When I got back a few minutes later, Shannon was sitting on the steps holding the crying kitten. I put the saucer of milk down and put Cindy's nose in it. She'd never had milk in a saucer before, so it took a minute for her to know what to do. Once she understood, she started lapping it up as fast as she could.

"Thank heavens," the judge laughed. "I was afraid I'd have to take Cindy back to her mother."

"She's going to need attention for a while until she gets used to being away from her," I said.

"I'll let her sleep on my bed," Shannon said, watching the kitten drink. When Cindy finished, Shannon put her back in the box and smiled as Cindy nuzzled the flour sack looking for the other kittens.

The judge had been watching Shannon with a little smile playing on his lips. When she stood up, holding her contented kitten in the box, the judge said, "We'd better find a litter box for Cindy and make sure she knows how to use it before she moves in."

"Don't worry, cats catch on real fast," I said.

The judge nodded and smiled. It's been a wonderful day, but we have to get home. I'll be in Effingham next week on a difficult case, so I have to do some reading this evening."

"Thanks for driving me home," Livy said. "I really wanted you both to meet my folks."

"They're fine people. I can see why you two turned out so well," the judge laughed and shook my hand. He shook Livy's, too, but I figured he did that just in case the neighbors were watching. After they drove away, we carried the food Mother sent with us inside and put it away. Then we decided to sit on the porch and talk to Duke and Stormy since they'd been alone all day. The late afternoon is my favorite time of day, and we sat there enjoying it, thinking of the fine time we'd had with Shannon and the judge.

The next day when I got home from school, I had a letter from Mrs. Ashley from Washington, D. C. It had been quite a while since her last letter when she told me about how well the film turned out. She'd taken the pictures to some experts to study, and in this letter, she said they thought the Lincoln letter looked promising. Naturally they'd have to have the original before they could say for sure.

Since Mrs. Ashley didn't want the Lincoln letter sent through the mail, she told me she'd wait until next week to get it. That was when she was coming to Chicago with Mrs. Roosevelt on a fact-finding trip for the President.

Mrs. Ashley's been a friend of Mrs. Roosevelt for years, going back to the time they belonged to a group that worked to get the vote for women. Now that the Ashleys are in Washington, she goes with Mrs. Roosevelt to help her on these trips. So Mrs.

Ashley said she'd come down to Marshall on the train before going back to Washington.

She also said she wouldn't mind if Scooter took a picture of the letter in case it was authentic. But she wanted me to be in the picture since I was the one to discover it. Mrs. Ashley's known Scooter's dad since he was a boy, and she was pleased I'd thought about giving Scooter a chance to write the story. Of course, she'd expect him to keep it quiet until she found out if the note really was from Lincoln.

When Livy got home and read the letter, she said we'd have to do some house cleaning before Mrs. Ashley got here. I'd been keeping the yard up real faithful-like, but I wanted everything to look special for her.

Now that the Ashleys have moved the horses to a big farm in southern Illinois, I hardly ever go out to the stable. But I noticed the grass around it needed cut, so I went out to look around. That was when I discovered the door was unlatched. When I went inside I found a lot of cigarette butts on the floor. I didn't know what to make of it since nobody had any business there. The only person around here beside me and Livy is Jimmy Black. He tends the garden, but he doesn't smoke.

After school on Tuesday, I walked home with Janet and Scooter, and I told him about the Lincoln letter. I'd barely finished telling him about it when he broke in. "How come you didn't tell me before now, for Pete's sake!"

"Hey, don't start complaining," I told him. "I couldn't say anything until Mrs. Ashley said it was okay."

"Yeah, Scooter, you're lucky Seamus even thought of you. He didn't tell me either," Janet said.

"Well," he paused to think for a second before he went on, "I guess you're right. Thanks, Seamus. So when can I get a peek at this letter?"

"Mrs. Ashley will be here next week, and I'd rather wait until then. I haven't even looked at the letter since I put it back in the drawer. It would be my luck for it to fall apart in my hands," I laughed. After I promised to give him a copy of the letter I made the night I found it, Scooter shut up about it.

We walked on in silence for a while, but Scooter can't be quiet very long, "Say, did you guys hear that the gypsies are back? They're camping out on the Farris farm west of town."

Janet looked at me uneasy-like, and I knew what she was thinking before she said it. "I wonder if Nelson Farris is with them?"

"What makes you say that?" Scooter asked.

"Well, I heard his father was one of the gypsies. When the police couldn't find Nelson, I just supposed he'd gone to live with them," Janet answered.

"I hadn't thought about that," I said. "It would be a good place to hide, and nobody'd be crazy enough to look for him there."

"I just wish there was a way we could watch their camp to see if he is there," Scooter said. "But it's out in the middle of a pasture, and there's no place to hide."

"Yeah, and we wouldn't have any excuse to be there," Janet said. "I mean, we couldn't claim to be bird-watching if they saw us."

"That's for sure," Scooter agreed.

Suddenly, I thought of the unlatched door and cigarette butts in the stable, but I didn't say anything because I didn't want to worry Janet.

"Janet, I said after a minute, "be careful about going out by yourself." I was just about ready to say goodbye and start home when I heard an angry voice coming from Shannon's house across the street. Then

Derek came out and slammed the door. He didn't even look at us as he hurried across the street and jumped into his car.

We looked at one another, not knowing what to think. Finally, Janet spoke up. "Maybe I'd better go in and see what's happening. I'll see you guys tomorrow." She walked across the street and called to Shannon. Then I headed toward home.

Thinking about the gypsies' camp only a mile or so out of town and the cigarette butts in the stable, I decided to walk downtown and speak to Chief Vaughn. He had told me after Nelson disappeared to let him know if I heard anything about him. So I decided to tell the chief about the stable.

When I went into the city building, the chief was having a cup of coffee at his desk. He stood up and shook my hand and asked me to sit down. After we visited a while, I told him why I'd come. He listened to my story real thoughtful-like, and after I finished, he got his hat and said, "Come on son, I think this needs some looking in to."

The chief drove into the long driveway that leads to the back of the lot and parked in front of the carriage house. Duke heard us drive in and came barking out to meet us. When he saw it was me, he wagged his tail while I opened the gate. Then he followed us down the garden path and on out to the stable. I shoved the door open all the way, and we went inside. Everything was just like I left it, so I stepped back out of the way while the chief looked around. After a while, he said, "It looks like someone was here quite a while from all the cigarettes he smoked." Then he stooped down and picked up an empty match cover from the floor. "Our smoker's been shopping in Robinson," he said, walking over to the window to look toward the house. "And he had a real good view of the back of the house while he smoked. You may be right about Nelson Farris being with the gypsies. I'll drive out that way and talk with his grandparents. In the meantime, let's padlock this door and nail that window shut."

After we'd finished, I walked back to the car with him. "If I was you," he said, pointing to the light on the pole that lit up the whole back yard, "I'd leave that light on at night. It might discourage visitors. And keep this dangerous watchdog outside," he laughed and patted Duke's head.

Two nights later, the stable burned. It went up so fast the firemen couldn't save it, but they stayed around to make sure the fire was completely out. Before they left, one of the firemen told us he was sure it was arson because he found a gas can in back of the stable. "It looks to me like the one who burned it left it on purpose, like his calling card."

The next morning, the gypsies were gone!

I didn't know what anyone else thought about it, but I was sure Nelson Farris had set the building on fire after he found the door padlocked. He probably felt he'd had the last word by burning it. But he knew he wasn't safe in town after the police visited his grandparents' farm. I didn't think Farris would take a chance on getting caught in Marshall, but I knew he'd never stop hating me for the trouble I'd caused him.

I was mighty glad I went to the police before the fire. This way, everything was on record for the insurance company. But most of all, I was glad the horses were safe on that farm when the stable burned. There would have been no way I could have saved them.

Later that week I called Shannon to ask how the kitten was. I was surprised when she picked up the phone on the first ring.

"Shannon," I said, "its Seamus. I called to see how Cindy is getting along."

"I was just getting ready to call you," she said. "Do you think she would like a little tuna, or is she too young?"

"Well, the cats on the farm eat everything from bugs to birds, and they seem to be okay. But since she's just a kitten, maybe you should just give her a little bit to see how it goes down."

"You're right. Maybe I should take her to the vet and get shots or something. She still wants to be held a lot, but she knows how to use the litter box."

"Cats are real smart," I said. Then I thought about the judge being out of town. "How are you doing without your dad? Are you lonesome?"

"Well, a little. But Janet's been spending a lot of time over here. And my aunt's here this week, too." Shannon kind of sputtered, like she was talking all around what she really wanted to say. Finally, she started telling me about her fight with Derek. "Janet said you were worried about the way Derek was yelling when he left Tuesday afternoon. She thought I should tell you about it."

"Well, you don't need to, but I didn't much like way he was acting."

"I didn't either, and I'm glad Daddy wasn't here to hear it." She didn't say anything for a few seconds, and then she went on, "Derek and I've been planning to go to the spring dance at the country club in Terre Haute for ages, but Tuesday, when he got so mad, I told him I didn't want to go."

"Oh, is that what was the matter?"

"Well, that wasn't the only reason. He's been going out with other girls. Some with, well, uh, some that don't have very good reputations. But what made me mad was that he lied about seeing them. I've always had this big crush on Derek, but now, I don't know."

"You mean you don't like him as much now?"

"I've always thought he was so perfect, but I can see he isn't. And after he lied to me, I told him I didn't want to go to the dance. Now he's mad because he has the tickets and has rented a tux and everything."

"Why doesn't he just take one of those other girls?"

"That's what I said. But they aren't the kind he'd want to be seen with at the country club. I already have the dress, so I don't know what to do."

"Have you talked to Janet about it?"

"Well, yes, but I still hate to disappoint him. I guess I'll wait a few days to decide. Thanks for the advice about Cindy. She's a lot of company. Bye, Seamus."

There's something exciting about seeing a train pull into a station. It's kind of dramatic, like an exciting part in a movie where folks have been waiting to meet someone they hadn't seen in ages. I was a little surprised to see Scooter and his dad there, and Scooter was carrying the big press camera. Since Mrs. Ashley's an important lady in Marshall, a story about her coming home was news.

After the conductor put the stepbox down, Mrs. Ashley was the first one off. She isn't very tall, but she carries herself like she was a queen. Well, when you see her, you're pretty sure she's the one in charge. She still has black hair, but there's a white streak on one side of her head that makes her look real different. She was wearing a blue suit and a hat with red and white feathers that curved down on one side. I figured Mrs. Ashley would stand out in any crowd, no matter where she went.

"Regina," Livy called. Then she rushed over to say hello. Mrs. Ashley gave Livy a hug, and then she waved at me standing over next to Scooter. In a minute, everyone seemed to be talking at once. Before we left, Mr. Schaefer and Scooter had made an appointment for ten o'clock Saturday morning to take a picture of the Lincoln letter.

It didn't take us long to get Mrs. Ashley's bags once Scooter took a few pictures. We walked down the street where Livy had parked her car and headed home. I could tell Mrs. Ashley was happy to be back in Marshall by the way she smiled.

The first thing we did when we got home was to head for the office. After she looked around, she said, "Well, Seamus, I can't wait to see the secret drawer I've managed to miss all these years." I felt real proud when I pulled out the little drawer and showed Mrs. Ashley the secret compartment in her grandma's desk. After I lifted the latch off the little nail that held it in place, I gave her the drawer. I thought Mrs. Ashley seemed excited when she took the envelope out. For a second she looked at her grandma's name on the envelope, before she took out the letter. After she read it, she sat down at the desk with a big sigh.

"To think it's been here all these years without anyone finding it." She put the letter down and looked again at the drawer with the partition that separated the top from the secret section. Then she looked up at me and smiled. "I'm real proud of the way you handled this whole affair. After seeing the letter, I don't have any doubt of its authenticity, but I'll always treasure it no matter what the experts say. Ever since I got the exciting news in your letter, I've tried to think of a way to show you my appreciation. So I've decided to give you this."

Mrs. Ashley took a brown envelope from her purse and handed it to me. I hadn't expected anything, but I was sure pleased when I opened the envelope. It was a war bond for a $100, and it was made out to Seamus Ryan Sanford. I was speechless. Finally Livy came over and put her hand on my shoulder, and I knew I had to say something. All I could say was, "Thank you, Mrs. Ashley."

"You're welcome, Seamus. I'm sure it will come in handy for your college education."

After that, Livy brought Mrs. Ashley a glass of wine to welcome her home, we had supper in the dining room. We hadn't finished eating before the telephone started ringing. It didn't take long for folks to hear that Mrs. Ashley was home. Her son, the president of the family bank, called to say he expected her to come for lunch at his house the next day. Then the judge and Shannon stopped by to see Mrs. Ashley. After everybody visited for a while in the living room, Shannon said she wanted to see the secret drawer and the letter, so I took her back to the office.

"That's pretty clever of you to think of looking at the back of the drawer," Shannon said, putting the drawer back in place.

"Well, it took me long enough to figure it out."

Shannon laughed, "Not as long as it did Aunt Regina and her mother."

I knew Shannon had something on her mind by the way she was fooling with the lock of hair that's always falling over her face. "What have you decided to do about going to the dance?"

"I guess I'll go. I wasn't going to until Derek told me he'd joined the Navy Air Corp. He'll be leaving soon, so I couldn't say no."

"I know it isn't any of my business, but I wish you wouldn't go. Even though he's Janet's brother."

I know, Daddy said the same thing when I told him I was going, but I can take care of myself," Shannon laughed.

That's when I got the awful feeling that something terrible was going to happen. And that awful feeling of dread didn't go away the next day. It wasn't until early Sunday morning I found out I was right.

The Red Headed Girl

Sixteen: The Accident

When I opened my eyes, Livy was shaking me, "Wake up, Shamie, you've had another nightmare." I was glad to hear Livy's voice, but I couldn't keep from trembling. This was the worst dream I'd ever had.

"Oh, Livy, Shannon's been hurt in an accident. She's lying besides the road bleeding. We have to call the judge."

"It's just a dream, Shamie. Try to put it out of your mind. If Shannon had been hurt, Richard would have called us." My mind told me Livy was right, but I could see Shannon in a long, blue dress with blood all over it. Derek was wearing a white jacket, and he was leaning over her yelling for her to get up. I could see his car, the front smashed against a bridge.

"It's not just a dream, Livy. Last night was the spring dance over at the Country Club in Terre Haute. Remember, you helped Shannon pick out her dress? Please, we have to call the judge."

"You're going to feel silly when you wake him up," Livy said, still trying to convince me that I'd just had a bad dream. That's when we heard the telephone ring, and both of us nearly jumped out of our skins. Before I even thought, I ran down the stairs to answer.

"Oh, Seamus, it's so awful," Janet sobbed. "Shannon's at St. Anthony's Hospital, and Derek's in jail."

"Wait a minute, Janet," I said, trying to catch my breath. "What happened?"

"There was an accident. Derek hit a bridge on the edge of Terre Haute. The police said he was drunk, so they took him to the station, and the ambulance took Shannon to the hospital."

"Does the judge know?"

"Yes," he told his sister to call us." It was hard to understand Janet because she kept crying and had to stop before she could get out her last words. "I knew you'd want to know."

I could hardly keep from breaking down myself, but I didn't want to upset Janet any more than she was. "You try to relax, Janet. Livy and me will go right over."

When I got back upstairs, Livy was getting dressed, so I didn't need to tell her what had happened. It wasn't long until we were on our way on Route 40. It's only fifteen miles to Terre Haute from Marshall, but they were the longest miles I'd ever traveled. All I could think about was I'd found my sister, and now I might lose her.

Livy parked near the emergency room door, and we hurried inside to ask where Shannon was. The nurse told us the judge was in the waiting room near the operating room, and Shannon was in surgery.

On the way to the elevator, I noticed the hands on the big lobby clock pointed to three. I've only been in a hospital a few times in my life, and it seemed like a tomb at this hour in the morning. The elevator door was open, so we pushed the button to the second floor where the operating room was located. I caught my breath as the elevator whisked us upstairs. When the door opened I could see the judge pacing back and forth in the waiting room. His shoulders drooped, and I've never seen anyone look so sad. He didn't know we were there until Livy spoke.

"Richard," Livy said softly. The judge looked up and smiled, then he put his arms around us both and held on tight without saying anything. Finally he spoke.

"How did you know? " He asked like he was surprised.

"Seamus woke up having a terrible nightmare about seeing Shannon in an accident, then Janet called a few minutes later, and we came right over."

"How is she?" I asked, trying to keep my voice from quivering.

"It looks bad. She's lost a lot of blood and has a broken leg, but the doctor's worried about internal injuries."

"How long has she been in surgery?" Livy asked.

The judge looked at his watch, shook his head and looked again. "It's been over an hour, but it seems like an eternity." He led us to the couch, and we all sat down.

"Do you know how the accident happened?" Livy asked.

"No, not for sure. A Terre Haute police officer called me and waited at the hospital until I got here. Apparently Derek gave them my number while he was having first aid in the emergency room," the judge hesitated a second, then added, "before they took him to the station. I assume he was under the influence."

"That's what you've been worried about, isn't it?" I said.

The judge nodded, "I should have put my foot down about Shannon going to the club, but I thought she'd canceled the date until Friday night." He turned to Livy and said, "I even thought about going myself, about asking you to go," he said. "Then I remembered the time I danced with you at the high school and all the raised eyebrows that it caused. If only I'd gone, maybe this wouldn't have happened."

For a while we sat there thinking our own thoughts. Then Livy said we could all use some coffee and went to look for it. The judge put his hand on my shoulder and said, "I'm glad to you're here, Seamus. I don't know how I could cope with it if…."

"Don't even think that way," I broke in because I didn't want to hear what I knew he was going to say. "She's going to be fine." I tried to think of some of the comforting things Mother says at times like these, but nothing came to mind. I remembered when I was worried that Shannon would never like me, and Mother told me that one day she'd need me and would be glad to have a brother like me. I wondered if this was the time Shannon would need me. I knew the Lord worked in mysterious ways just like Mother always said, but I couldn't understand why Shannon had to be in an accident.

"You're right, son. She has to get well. Did you say you woke up having a bad dream about Shannon?"

"Yeah, I've had several since I've been here, but this one was the worst. The others were all about when we were babies, and they happened on a train. I thought it was probably a memory of when Shannon left the train and didn't come back. So Livy talked to one of her friends in the psychology department at the university about it. He thought the same as me, that my early memory was what caused them." I stopped to catch my breath. "But this dream was different. I could hear Shannon calling me to help her, but I couldn't reach her in time."

"It must have been awful," the judge said, putting his arm across my shoulder. Then Livy came back with some coffee and we all took a cup. It was pretty bad coffee, but we didn't care. Sipping it was something to do while time crept by. After what seemed like ages, the doctor came into the waiting room looking tired and discouraged, and I didn't like the expression on his face one bit. So I wasn't surprised when he gave us the bad news.

"I've done all I can," the doctor said, sitting down across from us. "I've set her leg, and that will heal in time. The big problem is her ruptured spleen.

I've managed to stop the bleeding, but she lost a lot of blood before we got her into surgery."

"Well, can't you give her a transfusion?" I asked. I could tell my voice sounded impatient. I couldn't understand why the doctor hadn't thought of it himself.

"It's not that easy, son. Our hospital has almost no blood available. It's wartime, you know. While we have a lot of blood donated here, most of it is sent to the armed forces. Shannon has a rare blood type, AB positive, and we don't have any of that available."

"Well, surely, you have a list of possible donors," Livy said.

"Yes, we do. I've already sent out emergency requests, but it's early Sunday morning, and I'm worried we won't get a response in time."

"Test my blood," I said, jumping up. "I'm her brother, her twin brother. Maybe mine will match."

The doctor looked up at me, and I could see a flicker of hope cross his face. "How old are you, son?"

"What makes the difference?" I said, "Come on, let's go see."

The doctor looked doubtful at first, then he looked around at our desperate faces before he spoke. "You're right, son. There might be a chance.

But just because Shannon's your sister doesn't mean you have the same blood type." The doctor talked more about transfusions and stuff I didn't understand before he led me away to test my blood.

When he pricked my finger, I had a good feeling. Oh, I don't mean it didn't hurt, but I felt sure I had the right type. He put the blood on a slide and disappeared for a while. It seemed like a long time, but I reckon it wasn't more than an hour. When the doctor came back, he was smiling.

"Come on, Seamus. We're in luck," he said. "Let's go back to the waiting room." Livy and the judge stood up when we came in, and the doctor didn't waste any time. "Who's the legal guardian of this young man?"

"I'm his sister," Livy said. "Why?"

"We don't usually take blood from anyone younger than 17 or 18, but this is an extreme emergency. Someone in the family would have to give permission," the doctor said.

"Would it put Seamus in danger?" Livy asked.

"No, not really. He's a big healthy boy. He'd be a little weak for a while, but by drinking lot of liquid and taking some iron tablets, he'd be fine."

Livy looked at the judge, and they both looked at me. "What are we waiting for?" I said. "There was a lot of activity after the doctor took me into a lab and gave instructions to a technician about taking my blood. She fussed around with equipment that I didn't understand, but while she was doing it, she tried to reassure me that a blood transfusion was a normal procedure and everything would be all right as soon as my sister got the blood.

Finally it was done, and the nurse put a little bandage on my arm and left in a hurry. She wasn't gone for long until Livy came in and sat with me while I drank at least two quarts of fruit juice. I guess I must have fallen asleep for a while after that because it was light when I opened my eyes. Livy was asleep in her chair, but she looked up and smiled when I stood up. I felt a little weak, but that was all.

"How's Shannon," I asked.

"She's going to be okay," Livy said. "Richard's with her, and the doctor said you could go in for a minute as soon as you had breakfast."

As hungry as I was, I started to protest. That's when a nurse came in with breakfast for both of us. After a while Livy told me I should go wash up a little and be ready to go see Shannon as soon as the doctor came back to check me over.

I'd been in Shannon's room a good while when she opened her eyes and looked at me. "What are you doing in my bedroom, Seamus?" She asked.

"Don't you remember what happened? You were in a car accident," I said.

She looked confused for a minute, and then the judge took Shannon's hand. He'd been sitting by her bed ever since the transfusion and he looked mighty relieved when she spoke. "That's right, honey, but you're going to be fine now. You're in the hospital, and you've had a blood transfusion. Thank heavens Seamus has the same blood type. It saved your life." Shannon smiled a weak little smile and closed her eyes again. In a few minutes she was breathing deeply, lapsing back into sleep.

Later, the doctor told us Shannon was going to be all right now that she'd had the transfusion, but she'd need a lot of rest and attention before she was well. I knew the judge would see that she got that. He told Livy and me to go home and rest while he stretched out in the chair next to Shannon's bed.

When I came into Shannon's room that evening, she was awake. I reckon I wasn't back to normal because she told me to sit down right away. "You look awful pale," she said.

I didn't argue with her because my knees sunk right down with me. "How you feeling?" I asked. "Does your leg hurt?"

Shannon nodded and kind of smiled. Then she said the nurse had given her something for pain, but didn't say much more for a while. Finally she said, "Daddy told me about you. I mean, he told me you're my brother. I, uh, I don't know what to say. I mean, I haven't been very nice to you, and you've given me all that blood."

"Well, I only gave you two pints. That's what the doctor said you needed. He fed me so much grape juice I probably have more blood than I need already."

"Don't be silly, Seamus. Your body doesn't make more blood than it needs. But if it did, you'd have a real gold mine with your AB positive blood." Shannon picked up my hand and looked at it next to hers. She was comparing my long slender fingers to hers. Then she pulled a strand of her hair up close to mine. "They're nearly the same color," she said. I figured she'd done it to make sure what her dad had said about our being twins was true. She was quiet for a while, and then she squeezed my hand and said, "Tell me about us. Tell me everything you know."

"Well, I don't know much, but I didn't know anything about our folks until I was ten. Oh, I knew when I started the first grade I wasn't the Sanford's real son. That's when the kids started teasing me about being an orphan, but when I was ten Mother wrote to the Catholic orphanage in New York. It wasn't long until the nun wrote back to tell us what happened to our real mother."

"What did happen to her, Seamus?"

"She died after we were born. I'd always thought she didn't want me and just left me in the orphanage. Then the nun told us I had a twin sister that was adopted, but she couldn't tell us anything about you. She said when you were adopted, your file was sealed. She did send us a letter that our father wrote to our mother."

"What did it say?"

"He said he was getting a divorce because he didn't want a family. I used to worry that he might come and take me away from Mother and Dad. Then they adopted me and I didn't have to worry about that any more."

"Is that all you know about him? Is he still alive?"

"Yeah, I reckon he's doing pretty well for himself. I saw him in a Gene Autry movie last fall. He's a singer, and the nun said she thought our mother was an entertainer, too."

"Do you know what she looked like?"

"I've never seen a picture, but she had red hair, and the Sister said she was lovely and had a sunny disposition."

"I guess you get your disposition from her. You've always been so sweet," Shannon said, sounding like she was going to cry. "I don't know what was wrong with me or why I treated you so awful when we first met. I'm really sorry."

"Well, you didn't know who I was, and I reckon I did act like a hick," I said, hoping Shannon would stop talking like this. "But I was pretty sure you were my sister when I asked you to be my pen pal. Do you remember?"

"Yes, I remember. That was when we were ten." Shannon looked at me like she was seeing me for the first time.

"I've always wondered why you stopped writing. I sure liked hearing from you," I said.

"I don't know," Shannon looked a little uncertain. "I guess I stopped because that was the time I started taking ballet so seriously. I couldn't think of anything but dancing."

Tears started running down Shannon's cheeks, and she stopped talking.

I felt like crying too, so I handed her a glass of water, hoping she'd stop crying and talk about something else.

She took a sip and wiped her eyes on the corner of the sheet. Then she asked me to tell her what else I knew about our mother.

"I think she must have been pretty unusual. Her name was Marcelyn St. Clair, and at first I didn't think our folks were married because their names were different. But I learned in the letter our father wrote to her that she didn't want to change her name to his. Livy said she thought it might be because Marcelyn St. Clair was her stage name, and she didn't want to give it up."

"She sounds like a strong woman. Maybe that's why I'm so stubborn. What was his name?" She said it like she couldn't stand to say the word father.

"Michael Ryan. And if you want to know what he looks like, you can go see him at the movies."

"I don't care what he looks like. Daddy is the only father I want," Shannon smiled and said she was tired, and soon she drifted off to sleep. It wasn't long until I leaned my head down on the bed and fell asleep, too.

Later, I heard Livy and the judge come into the room, but I was too tired to lift my head. Even half asleep, I thought they sounded happy. "Look at those two red heads!" I heard the judge say. "I think Shannon's going to be awfully glad she has a brother. Do you suppose that makes Seamus my son?"

"I don't know. That would make Shannon my sister," Livy chuckled softly. "Does that make you my father?"

"I certainly hope not. For some time, I've been hoping for a different kind of relationship."

Usually when I'm listening to folks talk, I can understand what they're saying, but I sure couldn't figure out that business about the judge being Livy's father.

The Red Headed Girl

About the Author

    Ruth St. John Thomas was born on a farm in east central Illinois. She is a retired teacher and lives in Phoenix, Arizona with her husband and four cats. This is her second book.

www.ingramcontent.com/pod-product-compliance
Lightning Source LLC
Chambersburg PA
CBHW060923120626
46557CB00003B/861